Rose, the girl who loved troubles

A little thing written by Benjamin MERLET

Let me introduce you Rose. Her story begins in a bar at midnight. This plump thirty years old woman…

Hey! Hey! Hey! What? Plump? Did you just call me plump? No, no, no. I can't let you do that.

What are you doing Rose? This is my story, I'm the storyteller.

Hum no! This is MY story.

You're not in charge.

I can if you lie about my physical conditions.

Very well then, how much do you weight?

I don't know, I haven't checked lately.

Well I do know and I can tell you, and I can tell the reader that you should probably go jogging once in a while.

Ok… I don't want to be a bitch but I'm not going to let you tell my story if you talk about me like that, period.

Please accept my apologies beautiful, gracious woman. So, the story begins in a bar, at midnight, and Rose is about to be a little pushed in the ropes by a nice transgender.

No! For Christ sake! If you want to tell the story, tell it well. What are you doing? You're spoiling all the suspense! Now the reader already knows how it will end, what's the point? And how can you call the transgender nice? Did you see how she talked to me? There was nothing nice about it, on the contrary. I was the nice one and I deserved everything but rudeness.

My story, my way to tell it, deal with it.

Sorry mister the shitty storyteller, I think I'll tell it myself.

But...

Not a word!

You can't...

Shut up or I kill myself with a knife and there'll be no story at all, understand?

1 a.m. - a bar

My first encounter with a transgender.

Well, I guess I should introduce myself but hum, I prefer to jump straight into the facts. Right now, I am interviewing a transgender. The weird thing is that I'm not a reporter, I work for a movie studio. I dream to be a writer and, on the paper, I'm on the writer team, but I only do researches. A guy shows up with an idea, a cool t-shirt and a geeky face and says something like "I was going deep down inside my thoughts yesterday (which means: I was masturbating watching animated porn in my apartment) when this idea just appeared right in front of me, like a gesture from God, you know (which means: and I was high).

So, basically, this guy wants to do a drama about a man who wanted to become a woman his entire life and he has decided to start the process. As I'm not a screenwriter, my job is to go outside and meet some transgenders, getting to know them, their stories, the all package and to make notes about it.

And here I am, ordering a Manhattan in a flashy, pinky bar at midnight, trying to make eye contact with one of these beautiful creatures. It's hard because everyone here can see that I am the actual alien, they can smell my fear and awkwardness. They know I don't belong here, but what they do not know is my intentions. Am I a nice lost gentle girl who came to the wrong address for her date? Am I some weirdo who wants to make an article for a blog called "inside the human adventure"? Or, this is the last one, am I someone who wants to join their side and tonight is the night when I finally decide to show up and face the fact that I don't want to be a girl anymore, because deep down, I always have been a man.

Well, for the moment I don't really know to whom I can talk to. They all look at me suspiciously, even the bartender. There is no slice of lemon on my cocktail but there is one on the other's customer's drinks. I guess that means: *"go away, you're not welcome here"*. But I don't have the choice, I have a mission, something important to do, this is my job, and it is my job to convince them that my intentions are good and honest. I'm not here to assist to a freak show or to hold a Bible to their faces. No. I even recognize that their lives at this moment are better than mine, because they had the courage to be their true-selves and not pretending to slide gently into the schemes of society. Those ladies have balls, or whatever.

Oh my god! Oh shit. Shit shit shit. Someone's coming over. What should I do? Should I pretend to be cool, relax, at ease? Should I put on a happy and welcoming face? Pull yourself together woman for Christ's sake!

- Hey! (fuck, why did I say "Hey!" with this big stupid smile?)

- What are you doing here? (and she is not smiling... She is not even showing the smallest expression of kindness. Nothing. Just a blank face staring at me, making strong eyes contact, leaving me no possibility to escape or to back up with little proud).

- Hi! Well (would you stop smiling without any plausible reason!)… hum… I had a hard day at work so I needed a drink badly, you know what that is, stress and… (what I am doing with my face, am I Jim Carrey or what? Am I doing impressions?)

- Cut the shit. I know why you're here. (her voice is solid, steady as a rock)

- You do? (I am the worst poker player right now!)

- Yeah, this is obvious. I see it instantly, your shape, your bone structure.

- Wh…What about it? (ok, now I'm just confused… and I look like a woman that just spent two hours on a hard puzzle without finding the solution)

-       Come on. You want to be a man. You already have the body, a little bit angular and your shoulders.

-       No I don't! And... What? (and now I've got my crazy bitch voice coming)

-       Don't get me wrong. I'm sure you'll be a very handsome man.

-       But no. No. No, no, no, no. I like being a woman. I would never do something like that to myself. God no! (why did you say it with disgust... to a transgender!)

Superb Rose! You are doing very well! You were right, I don't need to tell the story, you are doing just fine! I love it! Keep talking like that to her and soon you'll be killed by an entire bar of trans.

You fu... No, no. I am not letting myself go wild. I can control my emotions and give to this dialogue a proper direction. All I need is to apologize to this nice and beautiful lady and you'll see, I will make her tell me her

8

all life and I will enter gloriously into my boss' office tomorrow morning! Wait and see my friend.

I'm dying of impatience.

- Oh no. This is not what I meant. I think you're terrific, amazing body and everything...

- So... You like me, is that it?

- No. I'm not... You're not... (this is a nightmare!)

- Well what? (she's getting upset and I will end up punched in the face by a transgender, nice work.)

- You are a beautiful woman and everything, but I am straight ok?

- ...

- Listen, we just make a bad start here and I want to tell you why I'm here ok?

- OK... (she looked at me suspiciously and she is moving a little backward as if I was carrying some disease. If there's one, it's stupidity right now!)

- Why don't we just give this conversation a new start. Hi. May I buy you a drink? (and now that I have all my senses, I propose a handshake and she accept it). I didn't even ask your name.

- Mila.

- Beautiful name. Beautiful.

- What's yours?

- My name? (Can you stop being so nervous! She is not going to bite you and remember, you have a job to do) It's Rose.

- Very girly.

- You could say that I guess, and it's not coming from the film *Titanic*, even if I could easily put my hand on a nice Jack!

-       Oh, me too.

-       Good! Good. See, we have something in common!

-       I would not go that far. So, what's your business? I can tell this is your first time here, maybe your first time talking to somebody like me.

-       That is correct. I'm here for work to be honest.

-       Work? Tell me more but before that, I need a drink baby. (to the bartender) Can you get me an old fashioned? Thanks darling. You want something?

-       I'll have a Manhattan.

-       And a Manhattan for the lady. (to me) Go ahead now.

-       Well, you see, I work for a movie studio, I'm in the writer's team and my job is to do research for the team. Right now, we are working on a new project...

- Let me guess, you're here to "study" the transgenders, you're like an anthropologist going to meet some savages, is that right?

- I would not put it that way but...

- How would you do put it? Tell me. Because, from where I stand, your movie studio is just trying to make a lot of money on the back of my community. This is just a fashion. I'm a transgender now for more than thirty years and I haven't read as many articles as today, it's all Catlyn Jenner's fault.

- Yes, but aren't you happy to be more accepted today than you were before?

- Oh my God! How can you be so wrong, so stupid and arrogant at the same time? You think our lives are better or worse than before just because every day I can see headlines about neutral public toilets or a special LGBT award in the movie industry? Don't you think we, all the transgenders in this bar, still get insulted on the street? But don't get me wrong, I never complain about my life, I don't go to places where I know I'll be in trouble, I know where to go, I have friends and family. Love, it's another thing, it has nothing to do with me being a transgender, I always have been a complicated person.

-        To be honest, I seldom approve my team's choices but it's my job. I would like to be a writer, to create and develop my own stories but I do researches. It has been five years now since I moved to Los Angeles, and the only thing I like about my job is meeting new people, going to places I never went before. Here I am tonight, talking with you and it's amazing. I would never have done that on my own, but thanks to my work, I push myself a bit more each time.

-        Yes, but your being here is for the money, don't make yourself a philanthropist or a pure, good soul. To me you're just as good as anybody else, or as bad...

-        Hey hey no. Calm down a minute.

-        What? Are you getting offended? You're going to tell me that you are here, trying to get information from me, or anybody else in this bar, just to be capable to go to bed tonight happy for yourself, thinking: "Oh Lord, I'm such a nice person, I can be friend with transgenders, those poor, castaway people."

-        No, stop saying that.

-        All I know is that you don't want to be friendly, you're falsely charming and nice just to give your team some valuable information about the LGBT community. You want so much to feel good about yourself, and you hate your job so much that you are acting like a mistreated creature. You want everybody to love you, this is probably why you're not a writer after five years of being the perfect employee. I hope you're not the kind of girl who brings coffee for everyone in the morning.

- I am (sadly. Oh yes! Sadly! She destroys me! I have been ferociously attacked for being too nice! It's not my fault if I can't be an asshole! My parents gave me a proper education and every time I curse, I want to apologize right away. Fuck. Fuck. Fuck! There it is, I feel even worse now. Do not cry in front of her. Look at your feet for a little while and drink your Manhattan without shaking.) I should probably go.

- Good idea and don't forget your priers before going to bed.

- Let me just tell you one more thing before I go. I do this job for the money, that's right, but everybody must eat, and I have my bills to pay, and even if I have my orders, I always put my best self into it. It's not easy for me to be here because there is a strong risk for me to get pushed away, but here I am, doing my work. I've met workers, nurses, policemen, firemen, homeless people, and every time, I've listen to their stories, I've put my all heart in it. I grow thanks to them and I will continue to, because I want to improve myself. I'm a nicely educated catholic girl, but I'm not a cliché and I want to erase my social and educational boundaries. I try to.

- What the movie is about?

- What?

- Tell me the story of your film. The one your studio wants to produce.

- Hum... it's a guy who wants to be a woman because he always has been a woman deep inside. It's a story about his battle, how he may lose his friends and family, stuff like that.

-        I really don't know why you need to go here and interview some of us.

-        They think the movie will be more valuable. You can even be in the credits you know.

-        Yeah, I always wanted to be famous, and maybe after the film is released, I could have my talk show "the incredible life of Mila, the sexy transgender". You know what your problem is, Rose? You don't really stand up for yourself. You try to convince yourself day after day that what you're doing is ok, but it's not. You're weak and you're being exploited. Exploited by your boss. Exploited by your parents. I guess you have trouble finding a boyfriend because you want so bad to be perfect for him, for his family that you completely forget who you are. Get out of here and try to have some respect for yourself. You are an embarrassment.

- You know, I didn't offend you, you didn't have to be so hard on me.

- I will talk to you when you will be ready. Now go home Rose. Go and sleep on it.

I looked at my feet and went outside, then in my car and finally in my apartment where I cry loudly. My roommate wasn't there so I gave myself up.

A disaster. The whole thing was a complete disaster. It's was like going into the jungle trying to catch an anaconda with a butterfly net. Not only did the snake swallows me but he vomits me with disgust. I will never go again in this bar and I don't know what to say tomorrow at work... Did I tell the story right so far? Is your book spicy enough?

You just need to close your eyes Rose. Everybody knows that, to make a good story, the hero must go through a series of events and some crisis.

So, there will be others, right?

Life is not a peaceful road.

I already know that.

Close your eyes and sleep Rose. I promise you, the morning will come, and you'll feel better, much better.

Ok. My roommate is just going home. I don't know where she was, I guess probably with Randy, her boyfriend. I quickly switch off my bedroom's light. I'm not in the mood for a talk. I don't have the strength right now to listen to her little stories. She is more than just a roommate of course but she has a gift to make things more complicated than they really are.

Don't worry, soon enough, we'll talk about her and her passionate life, and her boyfriend's life too, not that she is THAT amazing, but she really is something.

8 a.m., the following day a.k.a the beginning of all my troubles.

While eating a French toast, I'm thinking about last night. What impressed me the most with Mila was her composure, her presence. She moved as if every part of her body were in perfect harmony. She was moving effortlessly; her voice was soft and deep, and you would not dare interrupt her; her eyes were profound and powerful. She would strike you with her gaze, as if she were capable to plunge down into your soul. She was not blinking, she was the only master of her emotions and she always had a move ahead of you. But she was inspiring a strange feeling; as soon as you would see her, you would just abandon yourself, you know what I mean? It's just too overwhelming, too much perfection for a simple human being. I just wanted to be impressed, to be crushed, to be waved away by her. A doll in a storm. My words were shitty but I could not stop watching her, my defeat was something that I enjoy because I didn't even want to fight. If her kiss was a deadly one, I would have kissed her with passion. I kneeled in front of her and I happily show my neck to her to slide it.

I did sleep very well, and I feel refreshed this morning, but I also know that it won't be an easy day. I will, like every morning, bring coffee for the writer's team and I will only get one "thank you", from Frank. Frank is a writer, he is always calm and never get excited for nothing, he speaks rarely but when he does, his words are meaningful. He never uses words like "amazing" or "great", he always tries to be as precise and as accurate as possible. Sometimes, when all the turmoil in the room overwhelms me, I look at him a few seconds, to his calmness, he is my sunray through the storm, even if we never really talked.

You are talking as if you were in love my dear heroin.

Am I?

Yes.

My apologies. I have no feelings towards him, that I can assure you. Please try to remember that in this story, I am asexual. I am heterosexual but there will be no love story of any kind. Frank is a good person, the one that help me go through the day because of his good heart, but I don't really know him so maybe he is a pervert or some psycho. Who knows!

9 a.m. Walking towards death.

My workplace or the jungle.

Here we go! My workplace! Imagine a place where everyone wants to be. Willy Wonka's chocolate factory for example. Maybe you don't want to work there for the rest of your life, but don't tell me you would not love to spend a day or two over there. But, if your job were to clean up Wonka's toilets after he eats all that chocolate every day, well, maybe from time to time, you would punch in the face the hundredth guy who tells you "oh my god! You are so lucky to work there! I would give up my job immediately if I had the opportunity to work there."

Yeah, yeah, go clean up a guy's diarrhea every single day of your poor existence. So, that's basically the idea about my job. I spend most of my time in meetings where I don't have a word to say, my word counts for nothing, but my presence is mandatory because at the end of each of those meetings, my boss turns his chair in my direction and says "What about you Rose? Did you have the information I asked you to collect?"

When the question came out today, I watched all the writers around the meeting table and after what seemed to be an eternity, I opened my mouth and said: "Actually Bradley, I have some information. I've been to this bar last night, hum, this transgender bar and I especially talked to one of them, she told me her all life. It was fascinating and heartbreaking and…" but he stopped me and asked for my notes. "Well, I don't have the time to put them in order, we talked a lot, so I need a little time to put them in order, I hope it's ok."

It was not really ok. After everyone in that room looked at me in despair, Gary said he wanted my notes in the afternoon and a proper presentation of my so rich meeting with Mila.

So… apparently, I will have to go find Mila before the deadline and try to convince her to talk to me. No problem. No problem at all. I will be strong, I will apologize to her and... And maybe I can give her some money in exchange to her life story... Just a second dear reader. I need a milkshake and some fresh air.

You can't talk directly to the reader, you know that, right?

Oh, come on Mister the storyteller, we are talking to each other and that's pretty unusual, no?

My dear, it is completely unethical!

Who cares? It's a change, it brings a spirit of craziness to this book! Some fresh air!

The book would not need it if I could tell the story myself. You know that I am an omniscient storyteller, compares to you.

What does that mean?

It means that I know everything! Not only did I know what will happen, but I know every thought of every characters.

You're like a God or a superhero?

My dear, in this book, with this story, I am God!

And though, I am telling the story...

Well, sometimes, the creature is stronger than its creator... But don't worry, I am watching you closely.

Ok, ok boss. May I continue to do your job?

Please, be my guest.

10 a.m. The park (my feel-good place)

I sat peacefully on my usual bench, on my left there is the baseball ground and on my right a large grassy area where people throw balls at each other and where couples are lying kissing and napping, and next to me, on both sides of the alley, benches. I can hear far away the street noises and closer the game's shouting: "come on Bobby, hit the ball man. Your shoulders, be careful about your shoulders ok?" It's not silence, there is never silence in this city, it's a symphony, a daily, simple and pure symphony. Some days, I'd rather listen to something else, and some days I simply could not imagine hearing something else. I'm bathing in that multiplicity of sounds, it's chaotic but somehow all those sounds managed to form something coherent.

The sun is softly stroking my face. I know it sounds cliché, but it feels so good, sitting on this bench, looking to the others: the joggers, the dog walkers, the couples who met, the old man reading his newspaper and me, drinking my strawberry milkshake. For a few seconds, I stop thinking of the things that go wrong in my life, I stop thinking about my work, the transgenders or whatever. I just watch these people and I try to imagine what their lives are. Are they happy? The beauty of not knowing a thing about them is that I can create my own stories. Take this man for example, reading his newspaper. I guess he's about sixty, sixty-five, and he seems to be an ordinary man. He is well dressed, I can tell that he often comes here, he enjoys a nice walk, buys himself a coffee and the newspaper and then, he goes to the park. He spends an hour at the most here and then he probably comes home for lunch, or maybe he goes for a sandwich in a diner. But maybe, it's something completely different! When he comes home, he yells at his wife because she didn't clean up the dishes or because she doesn't take care enough of her physical appearance. This is the sad version, but maybe after reading his paper, he goes take his grandkids to school and buys them an ice-cream. Maybe he is a widower dedicated to his family. I like this little game, and I know that I can do it for a very long time. This is not the first time I see this man in this park, sitting precisely on this bench, we all have our habits, but we never talk to each other, why would we? Maybe someday I will because he will forget his hat and I will have to run after him and hand it back, and at this moment, a conversation will eventually start. But, until such a thing happens, I am free to create a different story every time I encounter him in the park.

Hey! Maybe I could make up Mila's life instead of going back to the bar. That would not be fair or honest, but I would go home safe, and not crying like a baby and that is something rather pleasant to think about. This little break gives me courage for the rest of my morning.

10.30. Looking for more troubles.

But what could I do with the rest of my morning? I don't think the bar will be open at such an hour. I could stay here a little while. I could go back to work, but what for? Hearing my boss' recommendations? Trying to avoid the accusing look of my colleagues? I'd rather avoid this embarrassment. What could I do then...?

I would not be intrusive but maybe you could pay a visit to your roommate. Because I know absolutely everything, I can also tell you that her bar is in the park vicinity and that you would be there in less than five minutes, and I can assure you that things will happen there that will make the story move forward. So please, go.

Ah! Not a bad idea! I could check her new shop and see what's going on with her, I don't really pay attention to her lately, so it could be the proper thing to do. Thank you nice narrator, you can be very helpful sometimes.

I expect this book to be sold, therefore this story needs action and it's not with you sitting on a bench doing nothing that it will happen.

It was a charming break and... you know what? Go fuck yourself.

Instead of insulted me, watch out for that truck, who knows, he might kill you.

Very funny but you can't, you need me alive.

You're right. I'll wait till the end...

Bastard. Cruel bastard.

And while you treat me like shit, look on your right, you are at destination. It's a pleasure to serve you madam. Rose, don't do that, put that finger away. You must act like a lady.

*

Indeed... The bar looks completely different. In fact, I don't think it's a bar anymore. I'm confused. Where is the sign? Where is the wooden deck? What the fuck happened? Where is the rock'n'roll and all the cool posters? The stage is still at the same place but everything looks so… peaceful. The walls have been refreshed, the furniture is different. Where is my old wooden stool where I used to seat? It had a perfect position, close to Thelma, close to the TV, but not too close to the entrance door. I know she wanted to change but I didn't know she was going to change everything. It's not the same place anymore. What have she done to my den?

-       Oh my God, you should see your face, it's hilarious!

-       Thelma! What the fuck? What happened?

-       You liked it?

-       Liked it? Well, Geez, I don't know. Give me a minute. But, wh… why?

-       Well, I changed the all concept of my business.

- Which is?

- Now, everything will be transitory.

- I'm lost.

- Yesterday, it was a bar. Today it's a coffee shop. Tomorrow, it will be something else. You see, we only use reusable materials. Everything can be changed easily at a low cost. The structure is made to last at least one year. If the business is good maybe it will last even longer, but otherwise, I'll try something else.

- But this is not a coffee shop.

- It is, it is. You want a cappuccino and a muffin? I'll bring you that. A piece a pie? A cookie? A cup of coffee?

- Don't you forget something?

- What?

- The cats! There are cats everywhere!

-       Oh yes, of course, the cats!

-       Why are there cats everywhere?

-       It's relaxing.

-       You are kidding me. Music can be relaxing too; don't you know that?

-       Not at all my good friend. Have you never heard of that? It's called "cat café".

-       Of course I do, but I never would have thought that you would open one.

-       Well, I like cats and I own a coffee shop so...

-       You owned a bar, with concerts, drunkards and... noise.

-       There will still be concerts, every Thursday, just like before.

-       Yeah, but aren't you afraid that this will make your usual customers go away?

-       Have you ever seen my bar crowded? Seriously?

-       Well, no.

-       So, a cat café!

-       And may I know how you intend to name it?

-       Meow.

-       You… fuck. No. You're kidding me again.

-       Nope. Absolutely not my dear customer and roommate.

-       Where did you find all these cats?

-       To an animal shelter. You see, every cat here is available for adoption. Do you want one?

-       No thanks.

-       Too bad. So, you see, I have done something good. I'm saving all these warm and cute animals, I'm feeding them, I'm taking care of them, and they will take care of my customers in return. When you feel blue, when you had a bad day at work, and I know that you know what it feels like, you come here, you drink a nice hot cup of coffee with a cat on your knees purring. I bet you can already see you there, a book on one hand, the other stroking a cat and sipping a delicious homemade milkshake. Imagine, it's raining, you don't want to hang out alone in your apartment, you want a place that give you the sensation to have a warm blanket on your shoulders.

-       So, basically, it's a place for depressed people, and you, you want that all the depressed people in town to meet there? And after, you want them to adopt a cat to end up alone in their apartment full of your fucking cats? You're worse than a pharmaceutical company. You don't sell drugs but it's worse.

-      Would you stop being so negative. When I had the bar, you never told me that I was making people drink. It's not because I'm opening a cat café that I turned evil.

-      I don't know. It doesn't sound like you, that's all I'm saying.

-      People change sometimes, you should try. How did it go at work?

-      Worse than never. I must fake some reports or find a transgender, or else I'll lose my job.

-      Rose...

-      What?

-      You already know what I'll tell you.

-      Yes. So, don't say anything please, would you?

-      Take care of you for a change. Want a coffee?

-    What about a milkshake instead?

-    No, you already have one.

-    How do you know?

-    You have a strawberry milky moustache.

-    What??? You could not tell me before? We have been talking for at least ten minutes Thelma!

-    No, you're cute with it.

-    Fuck you and give me a coffee, but with a muffin.

-    Go take a seat, I'll be right back.

She did a nice work. In fact, it's remarkable. She also got rid of that terrible smell. The smell of the bar that saw too many parties, but now, it's all clean, all neat. She must have worked hours and hours to get to that result. She never told me about it. I know we're just roommates, but I thought we were a little bit more than that after three years together. Maybe it's my fault, I'm not paying enough attention to her life and she's a bit mysterious to, she's not really a talker. She often goes straight to the point and I know she can sometimes hurt people by her bluntness. I think that's why I love her. Not because she makes people cry (me included, like that time she told me my rabbit was dead: "FYI, your rabbit died today, I didn't throw it away, I thought you might want to bury it somewhere in the garden so I bought you a shovel"), but because she is 100% truthful. She will never lie to you, for the best and for the worst, but she is my rock, I count on her too often, I know that.

I chose a seat in the back of the bar, where the light is soft, it's like a cocoon. There is a cat coming towards me. I'm calling him: "kitty, come here", making noises and trying to attract him with my hand. He seems to respond to my voice. I can hear him purr. Suddenly, he stops. His body seems to go limp and just like that he is motionless, on the floor. He doesn't seem hurt or anything else, but he is not moving. I ran to him in panic, calling Thelma in distress.

-       Fuck no. What the… Thelma! Something's wrong with the cat. Kitty. Come on, wake up.

I touched his body softly, he seems to be breathing but he stays on the ground, not opening his eyes, not making a movement.

-       Kitty, be a good cat and wake up please. Please, don't be dead. Thelma? Where are you? Your cat has a problem here.

Here she is, looking at me as if I had (again) done something wrong.

-       What is it?

-       This cat. He was coming towards me and halfway, he stops moving and… look at him. Maybe he had a heart attack. Can cats have heart attack?

-       Don't worry, he's perfectly all right. That's "Sleepy". The guy at the shelter told me he was not like the others.

-       What's that supposed to mean "not like the others"?

-       He has a disease. He falls asleep all the time and he can't control it.

-       You mean he is narcoleptic?

-       Exactly! That's the name. Sleepy is narcoleptic.

-       And of course, you called him Sleepy.

-       That suits him, don't you think?

-       And you are going to let him here?

-       Yes, that's better because if I moved him to many times, I forget and if he wakes up not knowing where he is, he might freak out.

-       Ok...

-       The problem is that he always wants to go outside but I can't let him or else I won't know where he falls asleep. Imagine, it's happening in the middle road!? He can provoke a major accident and I'll be the one responsible for it.

\- Well Sleepy, I bet I will heard a lot about you in the future.

\- There, your cappuccino.

\- What's all this on the shelves?

\- You mean the letters?

\- Yes, I was expecting books, you know, to go with the cats, the pie, and the general atmosphere.

\- There's Randy's.

\- Randy's letters? All of them? Did he willingly give them to you?

\- Actually, he was pleased for my asking. He said it will be an honor to have his letters being red by strangers, and that he was hoping that the customers will be moved and touched by his stories.

-       Since it's so hard for him to get published, at least he finds an audience I guess.

-       That's the spirit, but one day, his letters will be published. Enjoy your cappuccino and read some, it's really good, I promise.

-       Ok ok. Oh look, Sleepy is waking up! Hello little creature, you want to come... oh ok, go in the opposite direction, you furry bastard.

Sipping my cappuccino (damn it's good!), my eyes are increasingly intensely peering at the shelves and this massive accumulation of letters. They are all stored in small white boxes. Every box has a note on it that says what it contains. I read: "the story of Gerald", "the twins, Carol and Susan" and other names of unknown people. There is no more information: how old they were, where do they lived, what was their profession or what the letters were about. The only thing you could do is to choose a name and see if the story inside the box was good enough for you. Let's try Gerald.

While our nice heroin is reading, let me explain two or three things that she seemed to omit. You may wonder why this Randy has written so many letters, why is he writing and to whom? Randy calls himself an artist but he's not, he is just a sensitive guy, more sensitive that the average and, lately, Randy has a lot of spare time. Why you may wonder? You might know that later. The fact is, Randy decided to use his free time in an odd way. He looks in the phone booth, peaks a name he likes and writes a letter to that person and mails it. Sometimes he receives no answers but sometimes he does, and this is the beginning of a correspondence. Randy has some rules: never meet the person he's writing to, through Skype, snapchat, photos, Facebook or whatever. They know each other exclusively through the letters. Now, you might wonder about the content of the letters. Randy explains in the easiest way possible that he is just looking for human contact, for human stories. He starts by telling a bit about himself, he also gives his address and his phone number in case they would like to contact him. He writes between ten to fifteen letters a week, and some of his correspondence lasts for more than five years. That's explain why you can fill an entire shelf, and even more. In case you would have missed this information, Thelma, who owns the café, is Randy's girlfriend.

Spencer's letters.

Rose closes her eyes and picks one of the many letters in the box.

"June 25, 2012.

I wonder if I can talk to you about my grandmother. I guess you don't mind, otherwise you wouldn't have written me… The all thing is still very strange to me, but I must confess, I'm getting used to it. I'm 24 as you know. You also know that I recently got my own apartment, away from home, a step away from my childhood. Sometimes, I have this strange feeling that I'm murdering my childhood, erasing the tapes, something like that. As if there was an urgent need, an unescapable pressure from my close ones to grown up, to take my responsibilities, once for good. So, you push yourself to some changes, big ones and small ones. For example, I try to cook. I mean, cooking a decent meal, with vegetables and all the good stuffs, and I realize that I'm enjoying it. Some vegetables that I used to hate when I was a child became suddenly good to me. Their taste has changed.

You know that I always visit my grandmother once a week. But now, I am not as close as I was since I moved out, so I only come back once a month.

I always have been her favorite, for an unknown reason to me. I am not the last of my cousins, nor am I the first. Maybe it's because I was often sick when I was a child, and she was taking care of me while my parents were working. She was not much of a talker and it hasn't change since. But lately, she has been placed in an institute, for elderly people you know. She is no longer capable to keep her house clean. There has been a series of minor incidents, nothing serious but she was found by her neighbor at 3 am in the street saying she was looking for her children, saying that they've been taking away... Completely lost. It broke my heart to know that. So, I came to visit her, in her now home. She was ok, at first. But then, we went for a walk. Suddenly, she was lost. She couldn't tell where her room was and from where we were going. She kept saying the same things over and over. She was like broken and, at that moment, I realize that the grandmother I've known for years was gone, dead. From now on, when I will visit her, I'll be seeing my sick, lost, old grandmother and we won't be able to have a normal conversation, she won't remember the last time we met. And this is what I was talking about, killing my childhood because now, my duty, as for the rest of my family, is to make sure she is ok till the end comes. Our common duty is just to be here for her, even if she doesn't remember us, even if new memories can't be make anymore. Now, we have entered a phase of transition. She can go on for years like that, but it will never be the same. Today, what's left is strictly family business.

I think, and I tried hard to remember, it's the first time I'm aware that a period of my life ends. Even though everybody around me is trying to change me, in a more mature way, life takes care of that by itself, no need to be pushed. I can tell my mom: "stop calling me all the time to remind me that I must clean my sheets once a week". The coming death of my grandmother could be perceived as a sign send from God, or whatever. It's over now. She will never make me breakfast again. We will never celebrate another Christmas in her house, her old house, where my dad and all his brother and sister grown. Now, I must see her in a clean, impersonal, ready-for-the-next-one room. You can't make any memories in there, you don't want to. No, I don't go there with pleasure, but by duty, and I'm nervous about it, I hope everything will be ok, but I'm not sure anymore. I'm not a child welcomed by his grandmother on the porch, with a smile and some treats in the drawer, I am an adult trying to bring comfort and warmness to a dear member of his family. It's all changed. It means that now, I should not consider myself the son of, or the grandson of, but as Spencer. 24 years-old Spencer, with his home, ready to have his own family, ready to be the one giving, making barbecue in the summer, inviting my parents and my brother Dan. My parents too are getting older and I better be prepared. The other day, I catch my dad's look at my niece's birthday, he looked accomplished you now. He as the look of a man that brings his ship to the harbor intact. He looked happy, peaceful but also tired. It was like an athlete on the way to his retirement, he can still throw some powerful punches, but he can't long as he used to in the past.

I was never really close to my dad, I have no explanation, it's just like that. I never felt the urge to hug him and it was the same for him I guess. We are the kind of family where awkward talks and gestures mean "I love you". But, I know I'll be there for him in times of need. I just know that. I ...."

BANG!

-       Oh fuck! What's that?!? Sleepy? Sleppy! Oh, poor thing, come here. Don't you know it's dangerous for you to fall asleep on top of a bookshelf? You not hurt? Ok, ok Sleepy, go on your way, but stay away from trouble!

-       What was that? (Thelma arrives, out of breath, at my table).

-       Just Sleepy making his life as a stuntman, or should I say, as a stunt cat.

-       Is he ok?

-       I guess. He seemed a little lost, but he went this way.

-       I told you, this cat will be a source of stories and troubles!

-       He sure will!

-       Don't you have a job to go to or something like that?

-       Why? What time is it?

-       Almost twelve.

-       Gee! Fu..! No! Oh no, I'm late!

-       Time flies when you read these letters.

-       He sure did!

-       You forgot your bag.

Rose makes a quick U-turn and grab her bag. She throws a "thank you, good bye" while leaving, hurling herself in the street, trying to shuffle between walkers.

12h14 back to work. (back to jail)

Rose can't tell you but, believe me, it's a beautiful thing to see Rose running, zigzagging between pedestrians, crying things at them that they can't understand. I really don't know why she is agitating her arms in the air like that, maybe it's her way of warning people, it's just hilarious.

I am out of breath! And, please, stop talking instead of me, dear narrator.

Sorry, but you were running, and you forgot your duty as a storyteller Rose, which is, always kept your reader informed.

Yeah, yeah. Thank you, but I'm back in charge.

By the way, why are you out of breath?

What do you mean?

Why did you run? Why are you going back to your office?

Because, I had to... Because, hum... there is a meeting?

Is it?

Is it not?

Well, that was not the plan because it's lunch time, and everybody is supposed to take a break, but since you're here let's say you received a text from your boss.

Saying what?

"Where are you? Meeting at 12h, Rick wants a briefing. Don't forget your notes."

You have to be kidding me?

I am afraid I am not.

You're not a storyteller, you're a dictator who enjoys the suffering of others. What kind of childhood did you have to be so cruel? I bet you're living alone in a shabby apartment.

With a nice view on Central Park...

Listen, right now, it is 12h17, not only am I late for the briefing with Rick, which is – by the way- my boss' boss, but I don't have any notes! You know that I made that up! I've got nothing! If I go there with nothing to show, I'll get fired! What are you trying to do? Can't you right a good story without turning my life into a living nightmare?

A hero must overcome the events that come on her way.

But, you know it will be terrible, he is going to yell at me, he will humiliate me in front of Rick and in front of everybody, telling me that I'm no good, that he should never have hire me in the first place, that I am the shittiest employee that he has, that I'm an embarrassment for the company, that I am not worthy of my position.

Please, don't cry.

But you make me cry! You, fucking God writer, maybe I'm not real, maybe I'm just a character but I exist right now through your writings and I am hurt, deeply hurt. I feel things. Fake or not, for me, all this is real!

Why don't let me write the story for a while? Things are getting out of control right now.

They are because of you! You can fix it!

How?

I don't know, maybe the big boss has received a wonderful news just minutes ago, so now he is in a very good mood.

No.

Why?

Because you have to be hurt!

Is it really necessary?

Yes.

Is that what your book is about? Suffering?

No, it's about life-changing events, just like in Gerald's letter.

But I'm not ready for this, it's too sudden, too brutal...

Rose, I can let you write instead of me, but I can't let you decide of what is happening in that book. You are my character.

I don't have the strength to fight you, do whatever you want, you are the boss, another one in my life.

You have to trust me, everything I decide has a purpose at the end.

Great... I feel better.

1 p.m. Still alive, but in a bad shape.

I will take back my role as a narrator for a while, Rose is a little... how could I say that... knocked out. She has been pushed into a ring to fight an unfair fight, she had no way to defense herself and her enemies didn't hold their punches. But, surprisingly, Rose stood up. She was not defeated, she had the courage to ask for a delay and thus, she was not fired. Bradley gave her his address and a deadline, a real deadline: "6 p.m. this afternoon, my house, your work or you're done." You may ask why it was so crucial that Rose had her work done, why she is the only one to be punished. The reason is simple. Recently, Bradley had had a series of fails and he found himself in a tricky position. His next project must be big, it must be a success and a quick one, the studio won't wait months. Bradley has a lot of pressure on his shoulders and he has been a bigger asshole than usual. Rose happened to be the scapegoat. She has the meaningless job in the team, she is the one we yelled at, the one that responsible for all the things that go wrong.

Right now, after an hour that seems to have last an eternity, she has just left the building. She is ok. She has gone through a major storm, but she is still on her feet. She is a little zombie-like right now, but she is ready to keep on fighting.

Let's go back to her. She is leaving the movie studio with one mission: going back to the bar, find Mila and get her story. You may ask: why it must be Mila and not another person? Well, it's another trick from her boss. He wants her to get the testimony of Mila because he knows that she had troubles last night talking to her, so it as a way for him to put her in an even more difficult situation, almost an impossible mission to accomplish, but if she fails, that means she was not good enough for the job and that he earns the right to fire her, it is as simple as that. But, there is one way for Rose to consider this situation, let the pressure go because the issue is just too big. You could lose your mind in a position like this, your nerves could break down and everyone would understand it, but instead of becoming crazy, you just put the pressure away, you just keep going like you usually do. Let's keep things simple. Rose said to herself that she won a free afternoon, and she has decided to go for a drink. Mila or no Mila, she is going back to that bar and see what happen.

With a handkerchief, she removes some make-up marks under her eyes while walking in the street. She doesn't pay attention to the prying stares, her head up and her pace more confident at every step. I am giving her voice back because my dear Rose, I want you back.

Thank you, dear narrator. Mila or no Mila, I am going to drink several manhattans.

2 p.m. Back on the ring!

I'm leaving the sunny street and the white pavement to the inside of the "Blueberry". When you walk into a nightclub in the afternoon, it's like seeing the other side of a coin, everything seemed different. My eyes are assaulted by the raw blue light, and I can easily see all the shabby details that became invisible at night, the chairs and the tables all washed up, the floor stained from years of spilled alcohol and the not-so-red carpet.

At first sight, not a soul, except the bartender who did not notice my entering. He is cleaning some glasses while watching the TV. Without making a noise, I climb on a stool, he doesn't look back. I cough softly to let him now that I'm here and with a kitten voice, I whisper a "Hello". He jumped and the glass which was in his hand brakes loudly on the floor.

- Jesus Christ! Fuck! What are you doing here?

- Oh, I'm sorry, I didn't mean to scare you. You were watching TV and I didn't want to disturb you and…

- Well, if you didn't want to scare me, why did you go in at first? There's nobody!

- I know, that's why I wanted to go now.

- Wait a minute, I saw you last night, you were talking to Mila, right?

- Right.

- She's not here.

- I can see that.

- What do you want?

- Talk to you.

- About?

- Well, you see, I'm working for a movie studio and we are making a film about transgenders. It's a fiction and the hero is a transgender, the star of the film is a transgender! You see, nothing bad about them will be said or showed.

- And?

- And I've been very clumsy last night with Mila, and I don't think any transgender will be willing to talk to me about their life, and what's it's like to be a transgender, so I figure it out you might help me on that.

- They are my friends and my costumers, what would I want to help you?

- Because, if you care about them, why not help a poor little girl trying to keep her job, and at the end, a good film will be made about them.

- Yeah, maybe, maybe not. But if they don't want to talk to you, I don't want to double-cross them. I'm not that guy.

- Could you tell me where I can find her? Please. I'm begging you. (I'm pushing my boobs forward, making my deer's look)

- There is no need to seduce me lady. I'm the bartender of a transgender's bar so I'm not really interested in women, certainly not a Virgin.

- Please. (this one was sincere) And I'm not a Virgin, just respectable!

- (he sighs. He doesn't reply right away, looking at me directly, without blinking. If he has a heart, I can feel it slowly opens itself. Come on nice bartender, let your human side crawl out of the cage) I don't even know why I am doing this. (he takes a cocktail napkin and writes something down). Mila often goes there the afternoon, you should probably find her. If you ever tell her that the information comes from me, you'll be dead before you know it, am I make myself clear?

-       Perfectly clear sir. (I make the military salute)

-       Know go, I've seen your face long enough.

-       I'm not here anymore. I won't bother you again, you have my word of honor!

-       I didn't know you have one.

That was a rude word mister, but I didn't reply, I have what I wanted so, no need to make an extra fuss.

At last, good news today! I risk myself to smile a little bit, just to cheer me up a little more, who knows how long it will last...

I walk outside more confident than ever, heading to the address the bartender just gave me. Here I am Mila the transgender, I will plunge my bare hands right into your pumping heart and I will take whatever stories sleep inside. But, please don't punch me, be nice to me, please. Yeah, I'm a warrior, but also a fragile little girl.

I really don't know where this fear of being punched comes from. I should take some time to think about it.

I should make a list of all this stuff.

Maybe not.

There's too many. That would mean facing what's wrong with me. Do not open that box!

So, where am I? I should almost be at destination. Let see. Ahah! Here we are! And now, let find Mila. She must be... Oh!!!

Ouch! My nose. Oh god my nose. Come on Rosie, stand up. Come on, on your feet. That's nothing, you're not dead. Ouch, but my fucking nose hurts. That bitch. That fucking transgender bitch. She might have seen me coming. Well, that was not exactly a punch, but her purse is not a featherweight my friend, that I can tell you. OK. Standing. Wow. Take it easy. Can somebody please stop the earth from moving so fast? That's better. Thank you. Yeah. Ok. I'm feeling better. Oh shit, my nose is bleeding. I think I'll just lie down for a second. And... on the floor… again. You get the picture? My shirt is all covered of blood drops, and I'm trying to stop my bleeding with a handkerchief in my nose on the street. Can I check my dignity level please? Perfect, thanks. Can someone drive over me, please.

At least, she hasn't knocked down your sense of humor.

Well, today, it's all I have so…

You are a brave girl Rose.

I never take that as a compliment but thanks anyway nice narrator. I raise my thumb for you. What about now?

No, no, you're on your own.

What? You're letting me down?

You are the real storyteller of this book. This book has your spirit of adventure, your clumsiness and your honesty. I am just here as a back-up.

Not a God?

It's a role I don't want to play right now.

But can I have your power, just for a few pages? Knowing everything and all the thoughts, that stuff.

No.

Come on, you...

No.

But...

Don't make me do a blank page.

Ok man, stay calm. Let see, let see. Where can I go? What can I do? Should I go looking for Mila, again? Returning to the bar and try to get her address? I don't think the bartender will give me such a precious information... Another strawberry milkshake at the park? I need actions, I need ideas... The cat bar? To Thelma's? Can I just think of a place and be there in a snap?

No.

Not fun...

The "Meow" fifteen minutes later. (cool name for a cat bar, huh?)

-       Oh my God, Rose, what happened to you?

I can't see of Thelma's face how much she is worried about me, she is so readable right now, saying to herself: "Can this poor girl take a break from troubles?".

-       Believe me roomy, I have one hell of a day!

-       Come over here and tell me everything.

-       Can I have a drink first?

-       Of course honey, what do you want? A cappuccino? A coffee?

-       A whisky. Please.

-       I don't serve alcohol anymore darling, sorry.

-        This is the worst day of my life, officially. Come on, don't make me believe that you don't hide a bottle behind your counter in case of emergency.

-        You know me too well Rosy.

Two minutes later

-       Ah! Feeling better! Can I have another one?

-       You're almost drunk.

-       So?

-       So, you had enough. And stop doing your sad face, it won't work with me. Rose, stop.

-       But my life is a disaster, a mess.

-       Your life is fine, believe me, you just have a shitty boss. Sure, that's enough to make your life a hard path but it's certainly not a reason to become an alcoholic. I'm watching you young lady.

-       You're not the only one. I would love to take care of somebody, for a change.

-       Stop whining.

- Can I go with the cats and read some letters?

- Of course, you can sweetie. Take Sleepy with you if you want.

- You're the best. But no booze?

- No booze. You can have a milkshake.

If I can't see Mila without risking my life, and if I can't go back to work, I might as well be here trying to find some human comfort in those letters. But, there is still one major question: should I read Gerald's letters again and should I pick new ones?

Let's see the names on the shelf. Amandine, hmm I don't know, a little bit too French and too precious I guess. Mickey? I'd say a retire lorry driver sharing his road memories. Geraldine? Probably a young ballerina who craves to meet the prince charming. George? A World War II veteran. Olga? Sharing stories about her family history, how her grandmother came from Poland, Ellis Island... Why not... What about this one, Denisa. Let's

71

take a look. Maybe there is a transgender hiding in those letters. That will save my life!

Before I start reading the very first letter written by Denisa, my wonderful roommate brings me a milkshake and hot cup of tea, but I can't find Sleepy, the little devil must have fall asleep somewhere unexpected.

Denisa's letters

"I like your project. You seemed to be an honest guy and if I'm wrong, well... you'll have my life on paper! I never done that before, my older sister loves writing, she has a diary, many diaries should I say! Every year, my mom buys her a new one for her birthday. So, she is the writer in the family. Me, I'm more a Snapchat or Instagram person, mostly Instagram. You should think that I have no personality and that might be right, but I like the fact that you can tell a story without a word. I don't like the people who just send pictures of their lunch or their sleepy face in the morning. I like when someone try to catch a special moment of his day, for me it can be something as simple as my mother gardening in the sunset, my father reading his newspaper wearing the Stetson he bought in his youth, or my nephew on his birthday, smiling tenderly at his mother. It may look stupid to you... I want to burn my letter, this is really embarrassing, argh. You must think I am a simple-minded country girl with no friends, spending all her time with her family or on her phone, liking, tweeting, posting. The truth is I'll be leaving my hometown soon, for college. In one month, I'll be gone and even if I'm excited to start my new life as a student, I'll miss them a lot. I'm not the teenager you usually expect to see, I'm not angry at my parents, I'm not crazy about them either, I realized very soon in my life that my parents were not the heroes we sometimes picture them. They are regular guys, they have a job, not a great one but they always pay their bills. My father had an affair once, but I don't judge him, my mother has also her flaws, the bottle... My father never left her, even when she was drunk every Saturday night, and when she was trying to give her panties to a poor guy at the bar. He always tries to control her, but today she is "more responsible". They have found their balance.

I understood very soon that everybody is struggling, trying to make the best of everything. It is often very hard to just go till the end of the day, you must be your best self all the time and it can be truly exhausting. When you are a child, you look at your parents and you are convinced that they'll always protect you, that nothing can happen to you till they're here. And then, one day, you're fifteen, you understand why at school everybody tells you that your mother is the queen of the Saturday night. It doesn't mean that I can forgive anybody, I have high expectations. My parents have the right to be humans with flaws, but they have a family in charge and responsibilities. It's a good thing to be capable to look at yourself in the mirror, and not feeling like the first shit on Earth. You must at least try. I hate those who quit without even trying.

Life is complex, but I think this is why she is so precious and valuable."

Well, well, well Denisa, this is not what I was expected. I thought you were a Mexican girl leaving in a hard neighborhood, struggling to find peace and love in the middle of the drug dealer and the gangs. I'm kidding. This is not what I am looking for. Ok, now I don't look, and I choose a letter randomly, I don't even look the name.

Randolph's letter.

"My dear Randy, I have been deeply touched by your last letter, I would never have guessed that one day I would receive a letter and that a friendship would born of it. Because I can say it now, you are a friend Randy, we may never meet, that doesn't matter, I know in my heart that you are a good person and that your project is a good one. You are not just writing to gain strangers' testimonies, you try to understand, you try to communicate in a world where communication has become more than difficult because our ways to communicate has never been so numerous and yet, we never misunderstood each other so much.

I value your letters because, in a sense, we are going to what's essential. I can see your handwriting, I can see your hesitations and I can see when you are looking for the good word to write and when you are inspired.

How are you today? Did you have the results from the doctor? What did he say? You know, there is all sorts of tumors, some of it are harmless, others are real sons of bitches. It's not necessarily the end of the line, you must wait for the results. But, the most important thing that you must do is to talk to your family, they must know. It's a very hard thing to do, I know that but..."

I stop reading. This floor is spinning fast suddenly. I feel like I'm going to faint. I can't move a finger. I'm holding the chair as hard as I can. The whole room is just vagueness, colors, and shapes that I can't distinguished. I

don't even notice that tears are rolling on my face.
Randy has a tumor...

- You just read the letter, don't you?

I nod to Thelma. When she saw my reaction, she knew
what I just red.

- Now you know.

- But... the letter is from last month. How is
he?

- You can ask him, he just got here. Randy!
(calling him). Randy, we're at the back. Hi
sweetie! (they kiss)

- What happened Rose? You look as if a bus
hits you.

- Some kind of bus, yeah.

- She red the letter. She knows.

- I see. Are you ok?

- The question is: Are YOU ok?

-       Yes, I am. I am perfectly alright.

-       But the tumor…

-       I've got the results, it's was a small and harmless one, no need to worry, it has been removed and I am out of danger today.

-       Why did you not tell me guys?

-       I choose to tell anybody, except Thelma and Randolph.

-       Randolph?

-       The old man from the letter, one of my correspondent.

-       You told him and not me?

-       You know how sometimes it's easier to talk to someone you don't know – especially a correspondent – than to a close friend. I didn't even tell my family.

-        But they should know, right? I mean, there are people who care about you, a lot!

-        Now that there is nothing to be worried about, I'll tell them. I just called my mother to tell her that I wanted to see her soon.

-        That must have been so hard to carry this burden, almost on your own.

-        You know how Thelma can be supportive.

-        Yeah. Yeah that's true. She's our guardian angel. I feel so stupid. I saw nothing. Nothing at all.

-        When someone choose to hide something, believe me, he succeeds. And I truly wanted to hide my tumor.

-        But how could I not notice? You and Thelma, I see you almost every day.

-        We gave it a name (Thelma replied). We called it Bernie.

-       Bernie?

-       Yep, Bernie the tumor.

-       Wait... I remember you talking about a Bernie, that was the tumor?

-       Yes.

-       Fuck.

-       Fuck indeed.

-       Today is definitely the day God has chosen to check my heart. I swear that if tomorrow, I'm still alive, I'm running the New York marathon.

-       Randy, my love, can you write that sentence somewhere because we just had a confession here. Today, Rose discovered that life was not an easy journey with flowers and butterflies.

-       Stop saying that! I hate this fucking day! It's like I have been blind or asleep all these years, that I was fooling myself, but no one told me, until today. If I was such a foolish little girl, why didn't you tell before? Am I really such a spoil girl?

-        Hey, hey! I was just kidding sister! You're more mature than Randy and I, both. You need to rest Rose, you are exhausted, I never saw you like that, so overwhelmed.

-        Today seems to be the day where all I have built those past years is falling apart, so yes, I am totally freaking out. I might get fired, I've got punched by a transgender, and Randy had a tumor, and no one knew about it, how can I stay calm!!

-        Randy is cured. You are not going to get fired and even if it happens, that would be a relief, trust me. This job is killing you. This job is not for you. You've been doing it for years and each year, you seem more miserable than the year before. You'll find something else, I'm sure. If you are worried for the money, I can probably use an extra hand at the cat bar.

-       Probably, but I want to succeed with this transgender thing, I don't know why. Last night, this Mila, she told me some things that hurt me, and I want to talk to her again. We need to have a word.

-       Go talk to her then.

-       She punched me Thelma. Obviously, she doesn't want to.

-       Why don't you go back to the bar tonight? I'll go with you.

-       Why not... But, no. That's impossible. I have to see my boss at eight and I have to bring my notes, which I don't have because I lie.

-       Tell him you need more times.

- But that's impossible! Eight is my deadline.

- What if you make a deal with him?

- What kind of deal?

- You give him some notes that we will write together with Randy and you tell him that he will have the rest of it later, only he doesn't fire you.

- You really think I'm in a position where I can negotiate?

- Worth the shot no?

- Why not.

- Randy, can you help us?

- I'll make a round of coffee and I'll get my computer.

- Come on guys, I'm not a damsel in distress.

\-   Look Rose, Randy has no job at the moment, and I am not really busy right now. Let's do this!

I am really lucky to have them. They are family! First, when I met Randy, I thought he was some kind of loony with his poetry, the fact that he hugs trees to connect with the Earth and other things. Thelma never used me to see her with a guy like Randy, it was mostly bartenders or musicians, guys who loves to party all night, and who don't mind sleeping on your couch for weeks. But, we grew up, and Thelma has changed. Randy was lost, a newcomer in town, and he came into Thelma's bar to ask her for direction. He never left, and Thelma was seduced by his clumsiness, which contrast with his bright mind and vivid spirit. He is not impulsive, always taking his time to think, but that doesn't mean he is not adventurous. They are the most adventurous and open-minded people that I know.

Five minutes later (I have my team with me...).

We are ready, we are on! Thelma thought for a second closing the bar, but I forbade her. This is a not national crisis, just me trying to win a battle today (for a change). We've got coffee, Randy his computer and we all have a cat on our knees, purring and sleeping.

- Rose, you are the starter. You tell us what story you want to tell, what character you have in mind. Randy told me.

- Well, I really don't know to be honest.

- You are in this writing team for years, you must have thought of some characters in your head. You never thought during your endless meetings "oh, that would do a great movie character".

- Sometimes yes.

\-   Look in your hood and see what you've got.

Two minutes later (...but I'm still in troubles).

\-   Rose? You look like Sleepy, said Thelma.

\-   There is Don.

\-   Don?

\-   Yeah, but you must promise you won't make fun of me.

\-   You have our word of honor.

\-   Don is my companion, the guy I created years ago. He is with me when I'm bored.

\-   Ok...

\-   Do not laugh!

\-   No, no, I won't. Please, go ahead.

-       Don is a married man, but his life bothers him very much, he's not as happy as he used to be, his wife is overweight, and his children don't even talk to him, they spend their times on their phone and his wife is always posting on her cooking blog. So, when he's back home after his work day, he finds himself surrounded by people looking at screens.

-       And?

-       And he starts making up stories.

-       Stories?

-       Yes. Some skits if you like. It can be anything. Sometimes it's one detail that inspires me a whole story.

-       Go on, it's good.

-       In one story, Don has troubles sleeping. He is insomniac, and he spends nights looking at his ceiling. One night, he gets up and he is going around his house, looking at it differently. Everything seems different a night, it's all quiet and the blueish light creates a pleasant atmosphere, he feels alive, it's like a reborn. He starts making some repairs.

- Interesting and nobody wakes up?

- No, every night, he goes out of his bed, his wife and kids don't know a thing about it. He goes in the garage and he repairs the dishwasher and other stuffs. He starts gardening, small things at first, but then he becomes greedy, he wants more, but there are some risks because he doesn't want to get caught. He doesn't want his family to know, it's his private space. He becomes addicted to it.

- That's very good Rose.

- And one night, he goes to his neighbors' gardens because he knows nothing in gardening. He wants to see what the others have and what they've done. One night, he falls asleep in a garden but, luckily, he managed to go back to his bed before dawn and his wife noticing. He can't control it. Each night, the risks increase but he cares less and less.

- I think we've got something Rose.

- What do you mean? This has nothing to do with the movie my studio is making, no transgender, no life-changing events. This is not what my boss wants.

- Can you give thirty minutes and I will write something, ok?

- Ok Randy, let's see what you've got.

While waiting, I am playing with Sleepy. Thelma is busy with some costumers. I try to get a reaction from Sleepy with a plastic mouse, but he doesn't seem to care. I leave him alone and eat a cookie. The package falls on the ground, and before I can pick it up, Sleepy is on it, playing with it, running around, putting the package in his mouth, completely crazy about it! He is absolutely out of control. But, not only he is narcoleptic, but he also squirts, which means that sometimes, he jumps on the package but misses it miserably. It makes me love him more. He jumps on a chair, but before he's got a chance to make himself comfortable, he falls asleep and, by the same occasion, on the floor, sleeping like a log. Randy calls us, he has finished his writing.

Thirty minutes later (the needed time for my savor to arrive)

-       Ok Randy, let's see what you've got.

-       (clearing his throat) Well, here it is. I took some elements of your story and try to create one with a transgender character named Mila.

-       You're the best, honey.

-       I start. "Mila is born in a small town in Minnesota. A nice Christian family, loved by her neighbors and by the community. You could say that Mila was born to have an ordinary but healthy life. And she had. Until she was twelve, nothing seemed to trouble or disturb her. She was used to Sunday picnics with pecan pies, and she loved to watch the fireworks on the fourth of July. But one day, everything changed. When she turned sixteen, Mila, who was named Michael at that time, was raped by one of her uncle. It was her birthday, her parents organized a party in their garden, they were family and friends, cakes, balloons, music, children running around, adults drinking beers and telling dirty jokes. She didn't know if her uncle had too much beer or if he was naturally a pervert and a rapist, but while she was playing "hide and seek" in the barn with her cousins, she found herself completely alone. She couldn't hear any voices, no kids running or laughing, even the chatting was just a distant, almost indistinct noise. Suddenly, she was cold and afraid. She didn't see him coming, she didn't see his hands grabbing her, one hand on her mouth and the other on her butt. She was so scared, she couldn't move or speak. She lied down lifeless and, for the next twenty minutes, he did whatever he wanted. Someone called her from the garden, and that's ended the drama. Mila/Michael took a bus that night, with just a bag and few belongings. At the age of eighteen, she was living in Los Angeles and would become a girl at 21, a woman by the name of Mila. She never returned in Minnesota, she just left a note on the kitchen table that night saying: "I'm gay, I know it will be too shameful for you to cope with it. We'll see each other when God says it's time". Should I say more?

- Did you write more?

- I do, yes.

- Well, I love it, I mean... I... yeah, please go on.

- But that could be a start, something to deal with your boss, says Thelma.

- Yes. Absolutely.

- Should I pursue?

- Please, yes!, says Rose.

- The first two months, Michael was living in a shabby apartment, working in a diner. He couldn't sleep at night, afraid of sleeping in a city that frightened him and afraid of his nightmares. He became a night walker. About a month or two, he bought himself an old car and he started driving around the city, stopping for a drink or two. After a while, the city held no secrets for him and he had his favorite bars, one mostly. It was there that Michael met members of the LGBT community. Michael found light and friendship in Los Angeles, the sun and the sea healed him, but there was still something inside him, a disturbance that never left him: the hurling need to become a woman. In fact, he already was a woman but with a man's body. She had to be finally her true self and surgery was the solution. She was in the LGBT community and therefore she was never alone, always surrounded by friends, by her new family. She never spent a Christmas on her own, even if her family missed her. It was not the same, but they were things that she could not face. She bloomed into a beautiful woman, almost an icon to her community, though she never looked after fame or acknowledgment. The important thing was to be capable of walking in the street, her head up, with proud and dignity. At night, she loves to be attractive and glamourous, but during the day she is giving lectures on sociology. She has a PhD. The sleeplessness decreased but Michael, who has become Mila, is still going to her bar in the evening. Until today, this place is still her haven, her cocoon and whoever dares to threaten this stability will be fought hard. That's it. That's all I have written.

- This is perfect Randy! It was really moving. Thank you. Thank you very much. You saved me.

- A drink to celebrate? Said Thelma happily.

- I'm buying!

Randy sure has a writing talent. This is the kind of guy who should be in the writing team, instead of me. I left the "Meow" excited and thoughtful. Excited because I have something to show to my boss, but thoughtful because I wonder if it's the right job for me. Five years since I started, and I never wrote a line. There is not a single movie with my name in the writing credits. I'm an unknown artist at the best, a girl wasting her time at the worst. I want to resign but like a good soldier full of pride and devotion to her duty, I want to end this mission and I want my revenge against Mila. I will not let myself insulted like that. I will return to the bar. Wait and see Mila, wait and see!

Time to go into the lion's territory.

I'm in my car, looking for my boss' house, driving in streets boarded with palm trees, glimpsing not as houses but mansions, all more luxurious than the others. This is not my world, but I am happy not to be part of it. The streets are empty, and I know that if I park, in less than five minutes, a patrol will come and ask me about my whereabouts. It's a world where all the residents remain in their domain, hiding themselves from the outside world, partly because they want to, partly because they have to. In my street, there is life, people day and night, shops open 24/7. The counterpart is I must avoid some places at certain hours but mostly, I am surrounded by civilization and that feels good.

I always thought it was a hard price to pay for success. Of course, you live in a huge house, with a butler, a maid and everything, and yes, you have big parties with famous and powerful people. But I wonder how they feel when they are alone in the house. How can they not feel surrounded by loneliness? And when they are getting older, and that the phone rang less often, that less parties are given? I know that some of them bring their whole family, which I find a bit creepy. You can't turn your whole family into a business, it's not healthy.

You know that you are lost and that you are talking just to win times to find your way.

Oh, hello dear narrator! Where were you all that time?

Still watching you Rose. Keeping an eye on you.

Am I doing well?

I would have spoken to you earlier if you were not.

Should I thank you for Randy's help, for let me rest a little while?

Everyone deserves a break once in a while.

I see… It probably means that troubles are coming.

Rose, don't forget that a book is made of ups and downs.

I had the opportunity to see that, yes. But don't you think there is more downs than ups for the moment?

It's only because the final will be spectacular!

You know what? I hope there won't be another book.

Keep driving.

Fifteen minutes later (struggling)

My God, those streets are endless! Ah ah! I guess this is it. Is there a name on the wall? Somewhere? On the mail box maybe? Why can't they be like ordinary people! No, it's not the one...

Ten minutes later (still struggling)

Maybe I should just try a house randomly. If this day is getting even more stressful, I will not see the end of it, I'll die from a heart attack.

Well, I'm in front of Xanadu, sort of. This is not a house, it's more like a kingdom. There is a gate, and there is someone at the gate, in a little wooden house, a lodge. He is wearing a uniform, like those English guys at Buckingham. This is hilarious, I might get fired but what a laugh right now. I am seriously wondering if I'm not entering in another country. That would be a problem because I forgot my passport. Is my boss a king? My god, I didn't know he was that rich! Maybe I should take some pictures... Shit, here comes the guard!

- Miss? May I help you?

- Oh! Yes! Sorry, I was staring, this is so... big and beautiful! I never seen anything like it.

- What can I do for you?

- *(Ok, so he has not time to waste mister fancy pants.)* I'm here to see my boss, Mister Sheperd.

- I'm afraid you are at the wrong address, there is no Mister Sheperd here, but there is one three houses from here, on the left.

- You know what? That makes sense, because the house is a little too much for him and I always lost myself. Sorry for the disturbance Sir, have a nice day.

- Have a nice day too, madam.

Ah Rose, Rose, Rosy, you can't do a thing properly today. Beware of the heart attack. Let's see, three houses... on the left. That must be... that one! Ah ah! Yes! Less impressive, much more common, thrice the size of mine but not a kingdom, a little piece of old fashion reminding the glorious time of Hollywood. Must have been the house of a 1920's celebrity but not a hot shot.

No lodge and no guardian. Just a gate. I make my entrance easily, without meeting a single soul. At least, I know that my boss is not the kind who protect his property with an army of bodyguards.

I follow some distant voices coming from the garden, bypassing the house.

What a charming view! A beautiful garden, elegant and simple, and right in the middle, a stage. Yes, a stage, that's odd I must confess. A homemade stage entirely made of wood. There are two children on it, and from what I can hear they are rehearsing, they do a theatrical performance. The little girl is on the stage and his brother is in front, a script in his right hand.

The little girl is pretending to be a princess and she gives a powerful and passionate speech:

"Good morning to all of you, my good people. I am your princess, Irina de Drogador. I have been away from you for a very long time. I know that you have missed me, and I missed you too. There have been some dark ages, but everything is over now. The light has return, such as the peace in our land and in our souls. I know that some of you have betrayed our kingdom and thus, myself. I forgive them. You may stay inside our boundaries, but you will have to do as you are told. For a year, your salary and your profits will be the property of the kingdom. Those who have fought bravely for the survival of our nation will be rewarded. We offer you a land, this is your property now, you can do whatever you want with it, it's yours. You can sell it or buy some cattle. There will be no taxes for you for the next five years. The kingdom will be forever grateful to you.

She is bluntly interrupted by another character, which was not on the stage before or else, he was out of my sight. Oh my God! No? What the fffff....? I am speechless. This is just mind-blowing. I can't believe what I just witness. The heart attack may come, I don't care, take me, take my life, I've seen the most amazing thing in my life. My boss, dressed like a knight, making his entrance, shouting his lines. He is not playing, he is living the scene. This is intense. I should laugh, but I'm baffled more than anything else.

- I disagree with you, princess Irina de Drogador!

- Who's speaking? Who dares speak to me like that! Show your dirty face!

- It's me, Hubert de La roche fendue! I fought bravely for you and for my kingdom your highness, nevertheless I don't want a land.

- Why is that?

- Because I already have one, I will have no use of it. Instead, I want some medications for my wife, she is sick.

\- Why your wife has not been healed yet? Has she not been taking care of by our doctors?

\- Because she chooses not to fight, and therefore she is considered a traitor, princess.

\- That is correct. She is a traitor and you know that, so why come bother me with your troubles?

\- Because, I fought for you and I deserve some reward. Only you can change that decision. My wife has decided to stay and to protect our home, our land, she is not guilty of treason.

\- But you know that many have lost their property, destroyed by the Enemy and today a new land and a new house are offered to them, their lost has been replaced.

\- But we don't want a new house or a new land, the one we have is the best of the region.

\- Is that so?

- Yes, princess.

- So, you don't deserve it anymore. Your land will be taken from you and your family!

- What!! How dare you...

- HOW WHAT? How dare YOU speak to me like that! Hold your tongue Hubert or I will burn your whole family! You kept your house, you protected it because it's the most valuable of the region, which mean you have put your personal interests before those of the kingdom. Therefore, you are guilty too, despite your bravery and your accomplishment.

They make a break, I can see my boss' son giving them some instructions, he is acting like a real professional. My god, it was good, I'm thrilled. The little girl was so intense. And my boss! My boss dressed like a medieval knight! Should I take some pictures? In case he fires me... Rose, come on! Where is your honor! Well, my honor is behind my bills right now. And...snap! Beautiful! Jokes apart, I am sincerely amazed by what I just witnessed. My boss is a fantastic father, he built a stage for his children and they wrote plays together. It's incredible, he may be a shitty boss but he is one hell of a father! After all, he can be a good person, everything is possible. Let's go say hi.

- Hey boss! Hello! Waw!

- Since when are you here?

I really think that I must have come across some kind of transit point, and I am now in a parallel universe. I am standing like a zombie in my boss' garden while he is coming towards me dressed, I say it again, like a knight, and he has a big smile on his face, a very friendly smile. He is absolutely not threatening. This is so weird that I'm starting to consider that he might have a twin brother and that I am eventually in front of the wrong brother. Maybe I'm safe if the kids are around...

- Well...

- Did you see me play?

- ....

- Rose?

- Yes... But it was fantastic, it's great, I didn't know you were doing that kind of stuff.

- Nobody knows! And nobody will! Understand?

- Don't worry. Hop! Forgotten! I saw nothing at all! Please, don't kill me.

- You don't have to worry, this is a false sword.

I am not used to see him like that, I don't know if I have the permission to laugh... Dear narrator, was it absolutely necessary to put so many major events in just one day? What am I going to do for the rest of the year? You know it's only June, right? Ok, I must relax! This is horrible, now that I saw him like that, all the hate that I accumulated inside me is slowly going away. How can he have behaved so heartlessly this afternoon and now acting like the perfect father, and I can tell this not a mise-en-scène, they have done that before.

- Come on, Rose. I'll introduce you to the kids. (talking to his kids) Kevin, Suzy, this is one of my employee, Rose. Say hi.

- (both) Hi!

- Hi Kevin, hi Suzy. I really enjoyed your play, it was really, really excellent!

- There are things to improve, we're not ready yet. I could have played better, I know it, and this is not the best script Kevin has written.

- Well, you are very demanding towards yourself Suzy.

- OK guys, I must talk to Rose right now, so why don't you go inside and grab a snack? It's time for a good smoothie.

*

Kevin and Suzy have disappeared in their room upstairs. I am in the living room, looking at the family pictures. My boss, which name is Bradley by the way, is upstairs, getting rid of his outfit. Bradley married a beautiful woman, very gracious, with a kind smile and a warm gaze. There are pictures of their wedding, pictures of the children, playing outside, posing in front of monuments: the statue of liberty, the Eiffel tower, the coliseum. The house is elegant, but it doesn't look like a heartless mansion, I can see some magazines, children books or toys laying here and there. They don't try to spread the image of the perfect family. I have the feeling that anyone is allowed to let his personality grow. A real home.

-        Looking the pictures?

Bradley's voice startles me. He is coming into the living room, dressed like a normal human being.

-        You want something to drink?

-       I don't want to be rude Bradley but while I was coming, I thought I was going to be fired, and right now, I just don't know what to think.

-       I want to have a good talk with you Rose. So, a drink?

-       I'll have whatever you take.

-       Perfect. Make yourself comfortable, I'll get us some beers.

He hands me a beer and sit loudly in his couch. He looks perfectly relax, enjoying a refreshing beer. I have this odd feeling that I'm sharing a drink with my best buddy, but my tense muscles remind me that I am not. After a sip or two, Bradley gives up his way too cool position, he rises, looking straight at me, both hands on his knees. I can see the swift in him, I know he is going to give a speech, maybe THE speech. His voice is soft but deep.

-       How much do you like writing Rose? (*I was going to answer but he was not expecting me to*). Life is so difficult, it is sometimes so hard to go through the day that you have to build your own defense, you understand? Every day, I see you at work, and each time I say to myself "she looks like a deer lost in the middle of lions." Your kindness is your protection, I can see that. You use it to tell people "don't hurt me, I'm nice and I'm a positive person, I won't do any harm". Me, it's the opposite. Every day is a battle to keep my position, to keep my title. Today, at the meeting, you have pay the price of it. Today, the bunch has decided that you were no longer useful. You are washed up, we need another scapegoat. We need fresh meat and it's very surprising that you lasted so long. For that, I respect you. But today was execution day for you. It had to be spectacular and brutal. It had to because everyone must know that the same are upon them. You should think it's a tyranny and that, one day, I will burn in hell. You're probably right, but I have made my choice. I prefer to sacrifice a

Rose to keep my job than to rebel or try to change the system. I know I'll be nothing without this job, without being a writer. A few minutes ago, you saw me in one of the most intimate moment of my private life, when I played with Kevin and Suzy. This stage outside, we built it, the whole family together, we spent a lot of time to achieve it and we are proud of it. Since its building, Kevin and Suzy has written many plays and I have play a lot of different characters. We have a room just for the outfits, another for the settings. They also direct their own movies that we sometimes watch in the evening altogether. Little films that they make with their smartphones, nothing professional. Those moments are special, and I hope that my kids grow well and that, in the future, they'll be fine adults, respectable people. But I can't stop writing, I can't stop creating stories, it's like a drug. If I had to be a regular guy every single day of my existence, I'll kill myself. I do all that is doable to avoid being a common man. I wear masks, I have plenty of them. At work, I am Bradley, the son of a bitch, head of the writing department, I am a vampire who want to suck any good idea that comes from somebody's mind. I want to dive into the story and forget the pressure that goes with every new project. I want to be so involved that I can see the room fading and the scene rising in front of me. But I'm not the only one wearing masks. If you think about it, and I know you are a clever girl, most of us, we all wear masks. A son may not be the same when he is with his father that when he is with his girlfriend, on one hand he is the little boy, on the other hand, he is a lover. How many times are we pretending to be what the society wants us to be, instead of our true selves. And, I'm not even talking of actors like Jim Carrey or Daniel Day-Lewis, who never play but who became their characters. When you watch the footages of their films, you see how much they enjoy becoming someone else, how much they need it. They are addicted to it. It is easier for them than to be themselves, facing the real world, living the real life, where their next line has not been written yet, and where they don't know how the story will end. When I go home, I want to play with my kids. I don't watch the news, it reminds me how little I am, how impotent we are towards the events of the world. What can I do about global warming? What can I do about fires in California, floods in New Orleans? What can I do about mass shouting? So, I play. I play because one day, life will end, and I want to enjoy myself as much as possible. I play with my wife too. Not the way you think, we are very much in love. But, we endorse other characters' outfits, sexual ones. She is the slave or it's my turn, stuff like that. But, you see, the trick is to try not to play.

It's confusing I know. But, in all those games that I play, at work, with my wife, with my kids, I give the best of myself, the very best, I put all my heart and soul in it. I am not afraid to look silly dressed like a knight or tied and leashed by my wife. I have built a kingdom where the troubles of reality are kept as far away as possible. This is why I'm such an asshole at work. I need to protect all that, and these stories that my team are giving me, it's like food or fuel, I need it to live. This is also the reason why your notes are so valuable, because you, Rose, you bring me little pieces of real life, of ordinary people. And these stories, I saw them through the prism of fiction, so it doesn't hurt me like the news on TV, it does me no harm. I try to leave nothing out of my control. And do you know why I told you all this? Why you are here, in my house, hearing my confessions? It's because I know you won't spread them. You won't because you're not that kind of person, you have a strong ethical code, and you won't because the others won't believe it. I like you Rose, you are a good person but in the wrong place. I know you have brought me some notes, whether they are truly the confession of a transgender or notes of your pure creation, I know you came with something. But, I don't want to hear a word of it. You've been yelled at too much in this writing room. I already take the decision to fire you, but I won't let you go without nothing. I will give you some financial support and the opportunity to have another job in the studio, it may be not as well payed as your former one, but it'll suit you better. I know that right now, you feel pain and rage, you want to cut my throat and spill the blood everywhere on my walls, but try this new job, I promise you'll be happy there. I am not letting you down.

What to do after the storm?

I am driving to an unknown destination, not really looking where I'm going, not really listening to the music played on the radio. There is a storm of emotions inside me, everything is mixed up. I am massively lost, not knowing if I should be angry at my boss or thankful. I don't know if he freed me or punished me.

I'm living those kinds of moments where every song played on the radio seemed to be about me, about my life. Right now, it's R.E.M "Everybody hurts". I am singing. The more the song goes on, the more I sing loudly, tears running down my face. Yes, I'm doing my Bridget Jones, but without the ice cream, too dangerous.

The song ends, I park my car and I get in the first bar I see. I go straight to the counter, raise myself on a stool and I order a vodka. I am pulled out of my state of mind by the blunt voice of the bartender.

- What the fuck are you doing here? I told you I never wanted to see your face again.

- What? But I never...

And then, I realize. I turn on my stool and look around. Holy shit. What were the odds that I push the door of the bar where I was last night and this afternoon? But who cares now, I am unemployed, I can drink wherever I want, I promise the bartender that I will not bother any transgender or any other customer.

- I asked you a question. I have the impression that I'll have a lot of troubles with you. Can't you have some respect for people privacy? Mila already told you that she doesn't want talk to you. I told you to leave those people alone, but here you are, you didn't get the lesson hu? Maybe, Mila doesn't knock you hard enough?

- (I raise on my stool, pointing a finger to his face) Oh! Calm down mister bartender!

Enough is enough! I had a hard day, I just want a drink. Several drinks to be precise. I have been fired you know so, don't worry, I won't bother any of you costumer. I just want to drink on my own. (I calm down). Promise.

-        And you want to make me believe that you choose this bar randomly to drink?

-        Yes! It may hard to believe but that's the truth.

-        Well, I don't believe you. There are thousands of bars in this city, why did you come here, knowing you're not welcome?

-        (I raise again) You know what? I don't have to take this shit! All I've been doing all day is listening to people giving me lessons, orders and knocking me down. I had enough! I am free to drink wherever I want because I told you, I just want to drink! Look, you make me yell! Can a poor unemployed and single woman have a drink on her birthday?

-       It's… it's your birthday?

-       Here, my ID.

-       You should be celebrating, with your friends or your family.

-       What is it to celebrate? Tell me.

-       Well, a birthday is a birthday. Everyone deserves a cake and gifts and…

-       And a drink?

-       And a drink, yes. There, a vodka, on the house.

-       Thank you.

-       But, you shouldn't drink alone. Don't you any friends?

-       Don't worry, I'm not living alone surrounded by cats, I have close friends and family. Tomorrow is Saturday, so I'll have a party tomorrow.

-        Good, enjoy your drink then.

I raise my glass to the bartender and sip it slowly, remembering every words Bradley told me. Well, dear narrator, I guess you have one nice little story here. Don't you think it's a little bit like a soap?

Who cares Rose, if we enjoy the ride.

True. I hope the readers will love it. Time for another drink!

Five minutes later

Time for another drink!

Four minutes later

Time for another drink!

One minute later (are these shots getting smaller or am I drinking faster?)

Time for another drink!

Thirty seconds later (this is getting embarrassing)

Nine or a brother ring!

Rose is not... well, I think it will be better if I tell the story instead of her for a while. The bartender came to see her.

- Hey Rose, I think you had enough. You want me to call a cab? I think you should go home, take a hot shower, and go to sleep.

- But no. I want another martinini. Oups, I said to many « ni ».

-       I'm calling a cab, that's better.

She is now swaying on her stool, trying hard not to fall, both hands on the counter, with empty eyes. Someone is coming to her.

-       You don't look very well honey.

-       I just want another martinini. Martini! Mar-ti-ni !

-       What you need is everything except another drink, martini or whatever.

-       Let me drink alone, I ... Mila! What are you doing... I promise I'm not here to question you, I've been fired, so no more questions, no more inquiries, no more degrading meetings, no more punches..., well that's not a sure thing. You want to have a drink with me?

-       I'm fine honey. You mind if I sat next to you?

-      Yeah! I'll be glad, but I thought you hated me.

-      Obviously, you had a hard day, Billy told me you were ok. Now, I feel sorry for this afternoon. You know I'm a lioness defending her territory.

-      That's weird, I think I already heard that today. Is the world a jungle or what?

-      It's not a hazard if a lot of people call you "dear".

-      Oh, I never thought of it that way. But I want to be a lioness!

-      That's not in your nature, but you can be a deer who knows how to fight back. So, today's your birthday?

-      Yep.

-      How old are you?

-      32.

-       So young.

-       I'm not a kid anymore.

-       That's not what I'm saying. My 32 are so far away.

-       Feeling nostalgic?

-       No. Not really. Age is just a number, when you are healthy, of course, and when you can still fuck.

-       Agreed.

-       So, what's your plans for the night Rose?

-       Drink martinis.

-       It has been already done, you need to move on to something else.

-       Well, that was the only thing that came to my mind.

-       What about your friends?

- I'll see them later. What time is it?

- 9.

- It's still early. I'm hungry.

- How about a piece of cake?

- With you?

- Why not? Am I a bad person to be around?

- No. Well... when you don't punch people, you're ok I guess.

- You don't mind hanging out with a transgender?

- You don't mind hanging out with a deer?

- Rose, I think this is the beginning of a beautiful friendship.

- What?

- Never mind. Take your purse and come.

-        Where are we going?

-        Eating a cake.

We are leaving. Mila is holding me, in case I lose my balance.

Later, in a little place called "Pie-Bye" (cool name to, huh?)

Mila and Rose are set at a dinner table. Rose is sipping a cola, Mila a coffee. They are eating pies.

- Still drunk?

- No, I'm feeling better. The soda helps.

- Good. Ever been here?

- No, I never go in this part of the city, this is not my kind of...

- Of what? People? Environment?

- You know what I mean.

- Yeah. I know. I'm just teasing you. How's your pie?

- It's delicious! I could eat another.

- It's your birthday after all.

\-   That won't be serious.

\-   Who cares, and it will help YOU to get rid
of the martinis.

\-   Did you know that I went to see my boss
this afternoon and because I had no notes about
your life to show him, I made up a story, with my
roommate's boyfriend?

\-   How's that?

\-   This guy is a magician, I told him a story
that I wrote years ago, and he took elements
from it and created a whole new story.

\-   What's my imaginary life look like?

\-   I must tell you, it's pretty rough.

\-   I'm all ears.

\-   You were raped by your uncle when you
were a teenager, so you left your hometown and
your family. But, finally, you find peace and
happiness here in Los Angeles.

- From rags to riches, is that right?

- That's the idea, from the darkness to the light.

- What did your boss thought of it?

- He didn't let me read it to him.

- A real mother fucker, hu?

- Well...

- What? He too has made the travel from darkness to the light?

- Kind of. He has his points.

- Are you forgiving him?

- He made me a promise, I'll see if I can trust him. It's my only option to be honest. He promises me another job.

- What kind of job?

\-   I don't know yet. By the way, I don't know what your job is.

\-   I'm an accountant.

\-   What?

\-   You seemed surprise.

\-   Surprise? Well, I am baffled, astonished to say the least.

\-   Rose, be careful, you are going to step one more time in some stereotype.

\-   Sorry.

\-   I'm working for a big company and I'm making good money my dear. I was never raped, my mother approved my choice to become a woman, she was there for all my surgeries. I never had a real drama in my life, I mean nothing apart the usual things. I don't drink too much, I never do drugs, I love to dance and I'm particularly fond of karaoke. I have two cats and I love to spend my Sunday in my rocking chair, a cat on my knees and a book in my hands.

-        It's not what I was expected. I am glad to be wrong about you. I love reading to, but I'm not sure about karaoke.

-        You want to try tonight?

-        What time is it?

-        10.

-        It's early for a karaoke, no?

-        A bit yeah.

-        You know what, I would love to do that with you, Mila.

-        Good.

-        Could you just let me go home, wash and dress properly for the occasion?

-        I like that. I'll do the same.

-       We say 11? At the bar?

-       11? Don't you know how much time I
need to be ready for a karaoke night? Let's say
midnight. Your day of hard labor will be over, and
you will begin a new one singing, sounds cool
hu?

-       Sounds perfect.

-       Finish your pie and let's get out of here.

-       Yes mum. Mila?

-       What is it dear?

-       Thanks for everything.

-       You don't have to thank me. Ok, this
moment is getting emotional, I'll be waiting for
you outside.

*

*Back in my car, back in charge of the story. Back listening
to some music. Back singing, but this time it's "Girls just*

want to have fun". I'm singing, almost yelling, my car is a night club. I'm looking at the city, its lights, its stores, its people. There is a whole universe out there, good and bad people but who can tell the difference? I see homeless people, youngsters going to some parties, drug dealers, busy people going to work, people shopping, people trying to get a cab, people arguing, couples fighting, people going to eat in some fancy restaurants, people waiting to see a movie. I see ads, all promising something, but nowadays, we don't sell products, we sell concepts: happiness or health for example. You don't buy a car, you buy an object that will make you happy, something essential to be an accomplished person.

I see many people on their phones. I see heads looking down, to what? A game? Snapchat? Facebook? Instagram? WhatsApp? Looking to others' lives? And, quickly, I imagine what some of them are doing on their phones. There is this guy over there, his name is Mike (well, I don't really know but it's the name I gave him). Mike is on Tinder (why not?) and his finger makes this quick move from the left to the right, which means he is flipping through female profiles. Sometimes, he sends a "like", which means he is interested by a woman, but how interested? Does he want a girlfriend or a one-night stand? Let's see someone else, what about this little blonde with the red scarf and high heels, looking pretty. She is texting, with her boyfriend, making plan for the night. She is walking to her car, let's see..., she is going to buy a nice bottle of wine. She has the whole evening in her head already. First, a nice dinner, he is cooking, she brings the wine. They are not an old couple, so they are still things at stake, there is still the need to seduce the other. He has plan to cook his best recipe, and she wears sexy underwear. I know, it's cliché, the romantic meal and then the sex, she is on top of him, he is looking at her firm, well-balanced breast, he slowly puts one of her nipple in his mouth, licking it delicately, she loves it, she wants more. She gives him a blowjob, plunging her yes in his. On the dinner table, the meal stays untouched, the wine still in the glasses... They will eat later, in bed, still naked. Time will fly, they will make love again because nor her nor him wants to sleep. It is such a perfect night. Deep down, they are afraid. Afraid that they might never be as happy as they are in this moment. Yeah, I haven't had sex in a very long time...

Let's try another one. Hey, I like that guy! He is texting, and he is smiling. Oh, he is also looking around him. He is sexting. He is exciting by his text messages, but he is afraid of being caught. He is afraid that a person might walk too close to him seeing a dirty message, like "ouh baby, tonight, I'm going to spank your ass so hard". Maybe, he has send to the girl a dirty picture. Come on, Rose. Calm down, the guy is on the street, I hope he didn't undressed in the street. No, no. I know! He has received a dirty picture, that's why he is smiling so much and that's why he is also so shy. The little bastard, and he is hard right now and he hopes nobody will notice it. My God, this is good. But, the girl is not available tonight (that's right dear reader, not everybody can have sex tonight), she has a girl night and she can't cancel it *because it has been so long since they all have a party together. They will send each other hot text messages all night, her friends will be unhappy to see her smiling about "nothing" and he, alone in his apartment, well... he will masturbate a lot! There will be...*

STOP! Stop Rose. This is not "Fifty shades of Grey". I promise Rose, if you continue with your sex stories, I will write something dirty: a whole bunch of miners coming to town, you have a flat tire, you pull over, the all bunch comes to help you, you are all aroused by their masculine presence and, suddenly, you give yourself up to all this men, you let them do whatever they want with your body, a hundred men! They all want their turn! They all want to cum!

STOP! Jesus Christ, ok! You don't have to be so brutal. You know what, you've ruined my game. Luckily for you, I just got home.

Don't do that again! This is not a pornographic novel!

Come on, the reader deserves a little nipple from time to time.

Not in my book!

Alright... I give up. You don't want to see a woman's body, but you are ok with her being punched in the face. Nice. Very nice.

Don't draw such quick conclusions Rose, I...

You know what? I was trying to be funny. I was trying to lighten my mood. And you know it because you are in my head, you know by advance everything that is happening in this book, so you know that all I am thinking is: I don't have a job anymore. I have been fire and despite all the comforting sentences of my boss, I can't get out of my head the idea that I failed. I failed. I wanted to be a writer. Everything is happening so fast, I didn't have the time to think about it. I am fired. I have been fired. Tomorrow, I won't get up at 7 like I did for the past five years. I won't buy coffee for the team. I won't go in the park at lunch. I won't be walking between sets in the studio anymore. I won't have to create stories anymore. I won't have to be creative anymore. I don't know what I can do. Bradley promises me another job, but how can he know what's good for me? I am lost, completely lost. What am I doing? I was fired in the afternoon and tonight I want to go singing? What am I thinking? I should better go early and tomorrow morning, at eight sharp, I'll go see Bradley.

10h30. My apartment (where the craziness goes on).

The end is near.

As I'm climbing the stairs leading to my apartment, I can hear some unusual noise, coming from the top. The more I climb, the more the noise is persistent. It's people talking, chatting loudly. But, what I can't figure out, is how many they are. From what I hear, it's a whole crowd up there! Is Thelma having a party? She didn't tell me. When I arrived to the 6th floor, I discover people everywhere. Countless people with drinks in their hands, talking warmly, laughing and hugging. I am confused. Who are they? What are they doing in my place? Ok, at first sight, they don't seem dangerous. They look really nice actually. Warm people as it seems, and suddenly, out of nowhere, I can feel, growing in me the urge to go talk to them and why not, have a few hugs. As I enter my apartment, I must find a way in through all this people, and as I move into, I meet nothing but warm smiles, nice

faces saying "hi", "how are you?". I try to find Thelma.
Finally, I see Randy in the kitchen and go directly to him.

- Randy! Randy! What's going on? Who are all these people?

- Rose, it's amazing! It's absolutely incredible!

- Why? What? What is it?

- My correspondents!

- What?

- They are all my correspondents! They all came!

- You mean that all these people are the ones you are writing to?

- Yes!

- How did they get there? And, you didn't know they were coming?

- It was all part of Randolph's plan!

-      Who's Randolph?

-      The one I told about my tumor.

-      I didn't know that your correspondents know each other.

-      I didn't know either, but as I told you, it's Randolph who wrote to Thelma and Thelma gave him the address of all my correspondents. And... I still can't believe it, but they came! They came for me Rose.

-      My God, Randy. This is... I mean... I can't even find the words.

-      I know Rose. Robert told me they wanted to thank me for what I did, for my letters and that they wanted to be there for me, even if I'm out of danger today.

-      This is beautiful Randy. They are so many people, it is incredible. How many are they?

-      47.

-       I didn't know that our apartment could welcome so many people, that's good to know!

-       And they brought drinks and food.

-       That's swell because I need a drink. I dreamed to have a drink the entire day.

-       Are you ok Rose?

-       I'll tell you what, this makes me believe again in mankind.

-       Yes. A drink Rose?

-       With pleasure!

-       What do you want?

-       I don't know, but I know what I don't want!

*

I'm in the bathroom, washing my face, enjoying a moment of peace. What a night, and what a day. I feel exhausted. The day is almost over. I sip my drink peacefully and I can feel that my troubles are coming to an end – at least for today - what a rel...

- Sleepy!!!

I jump, I scream, and I spill my drink all over the floor. Why on earth did Thelma scream like that? I storm out of the bathroom and catch Thelma, running in the hallway.

- Thelma! Thelma. *I am trying to calm her down, she has her crazy look and she is searching everywhere, like a mad woman.* What are you doing? *She tries to escape but I hold her back by the harm.* Hold still. Please!

- I can't. You don't understand, I can't. Let me go Rose.

- Thelma! Look at me! What is it?

- It's Sleepy, I can't find him.

- Does he not spend the night at the café?

- Not Sleepy, he must be watched all the time.

145

-        He must have fall asleep somewhere, it's his specialty.

-        No, no. He's not here.

-        How can you be so sure he's not here? They are about fifty people here, he must have gone in a nice quiet corner. Have you check under the beds or in your wardrobe?

-        Yes, I've already done that, he's not there. He's just a baby and he's helpless. Can you help me find him Rose?

-        After all you've done for me today…

-        We must try to figure out where he could have go.

-        With the crowd in here, maybe he left the apartment, that means he could have gone anywhere in the building, on the roof, in the basement and even in the street.

-        We need help.

- Well, we've got plenty of people at our disposal.

- Oh my God, yes!

Like a General, Thelma, standing up on our dinner table, gave orders and directions to the cheerful band gathered in our apartment. She was firm and clear, we have made groups of five and each group had its location to search. I have been assigned to the roof with two companions: Mona and Billy, a sixty years old couple from Minnesota. We have plenty of space to search, our roof is huge, and through the years, people get used to put their old bikes, tools, and other stuffs here. It's pretty much like an open dumping. As we are looking under every box, the three of us chat. Mona and Billy are married for forty years, they have five children and seven grandchildren. They came because they were touched by Randy's letters and because five years ago, Mona had breast cancer. Today, it's just a bad memory but she wanted to be there for

Randy, to show him her support. An ordinary couple, they didn't travel much because they had to feed the kids and pay the bills. Today, they are on the rim of retirement, Billy is still a career counselor, but he is a bit tired of the today's youth. Mona is a secretary, the best of the company, her boss, the CEO, would not let her go for all the money in the world. She never forgets a thing and she knows by heart all the needs of her boss and colleagues. More than a secretary, she is the mother of the entire company, never looking for fame or any kind of acknowledgment. Bobby told me that when she was sick, she had to be away from work for about two months. And Billy told me that during her sick leave, the company was a mess and when she came back, she found her boss crying in his office, almost making a nervous breakdown.

They both work hard and they both never complain. But, almost whispering, Mona told me like a confession that two years ago, when they were sure she was cured from cancer, Billy set off. He left the house one morning and came back four months later. He made a trip in the Appalachians, he needed to reconnect himself to the Earth, to the simple things. She forgave him because when he came back, and she always knew he will come back, Billy was in love, madly in love again. During this four months, they both have slept with other people. I was shocked by what Mona told me. Then, she said to me that they had no secret for each other, they had been honest since the first day. They even share their bed stories, what they felt having sex with others, they laughed, and they cried. But, they are in love, just like the first day. And the sex, Mona told me, better than ever… Billy shouts from the far end of the roof that he could not agree more. We all laughed.

Later on, I was sitting on the roof's rim, looking down to the countless little figures, Randy's friends, looking for Sleepy with their lights. The air was cool. I saw Thelma, looking with so much fervor that I felt guilty. Back to work Rosy!

Let think for a second... If I were a cat, where would I go? But Sleepy is no ordinary cat, he is a cat who can fall asleep at any second. Come on, think like a cat Rose. Cats like to climb... Did I check the trees in front of the building? What an idiot, I completely forgot the trees! Sleepy, kitty! Where are... Oh my god! Oh no! Sleepy!

I am running downstairs, I need to catch Thelma as fast as I can. I reach her, out of breath.

- Thelma, I have find the little devil.

- Where is he?

- Come with me!

And I run back. Thelma is following me, asking me again where Sleepy is, but I don't have the time to answer her. We need to rush, he might fall at any moment. Randy catches us running in the stairs and he follows us.

- Girls?! Thelma, Rose? Where are running like that?

-      Rose won't tell me but I think she has found Sleepy.

-      But where?

-      I told you she didn't tell me Randy!

At last, we arrived on the roof. I point my finger to one of the trees.

-      Here! Sleepy fell asleep on a branch.

-      Oh no!

-      I'm calling the firemen, they are the only one who can reach him with their ladder.

-      Good idea Randy. Thelma, what are you doing?

-      I can go and fetch him myself. I'm sure I can do it.

-      No, you can't! Do you want to kill yourself!

-      But it's my cat.

- Listen Thelma, if you wake him up, if you frighten him, he will fall, and he will kill himself. Is that what you want?

- But he needs me. I could jump or...

- What do you mean jump? Since when you are Michael Jordan?

- (Randy gets back to us) Bad news, the firemen won't come here soon, a fire just started in a factory and they only take real emergencies.

- But this is an emergency! Poor Sleepy!

- I know what we can do. I have an idea

The three of us look back to see Billy behind us.

- Please, Billy, we don't ask for your help.

- Rose, I have been a volunteer fireman, I have experience.

- Ok Bill, what's your big idea?

\-   There is a ladder over there, big enough to reach the cat from the roof.

\-   What do you mean from the roof? (*I wonder if Bobby was not a daredevil in his youth*).

\-   Get all the people on the roof. We will hold the ladder horizontally and someone will use it to reach the cat.

\-   That doesn't seem to be a bad idea...

\-   I go fetch the ladder, you tell everybody to get up here.

Five minutes later (it's crazy how time flies in this book!)

We are now divided into two groups. One group on the street with a stretched sheet in case Sleepy fell. One group on the roof holding tight the ladder. Thelma is the one walking, or should I say crawling on the ladder. Sleepy is still asleep which make things easier because we are afraid that if he is waking up, he might freak out to see that he is so high in the tree, or he might just make a clumsy movement and fall. The ladder doesn't touch the tree, so Thelma's moves don't impact the tree. We are all looking in the same direction, everyone is absolutely silent, all we can ear are the city's noises, the ambulance hurling far away, the traffic or the wind. Thelma is moving slowly, cautiously. I hold my breath, everyone is. Thelma can almost touch Sleepy. Out of nowhere, we hear a man in the street shouting: "Hey, what are doing up here?". We all startle. The ladder remains steady, but Thelma nearly lost her balance. She can't help but shouting back at the man "Go buy yourself another beer you drunk, but if I hear you scream again, I swear to God, I cut you into tiny pieces that I will spread all over the city." The man is quickly going the other way. Thelma is moving again. She is almost at reach. She must act fast because Sleepy is waking up, his little body moving to the left. Thelma rises her hand and catches Sleepy a second before he fells. Everyone relax a little, I can almost hear forty-seven hearts beating anew. She grabs him by the neck, half of her body suspended in the air.

-        Hold your cat Thelma, we are going to pull back the ladder, Billy shouts at her.

Like one man, we all gathered our strength and we pull Thelma and Sleepy to the roof. Safely, they both return to the building. Thelma is holding Sleepy against her, and even if he seems to be safe, she refuses to loosen her embrace. I decide to utter the proper sentence for such a moment.

-        Let's go have a drink to celebrate!

The cheers from the group are the perfect answer. This is the perfect end for a tough day. But, I can't rest very long, my phone is ringing. It's Mila. Mila! Dawn, I forgot.

- Mila, sorry!

- My dear, I thought we were friend, how come you're not here? Is it the fault of the Martinis?

- No, it's a crazy story, my roommate's cat was trapped in a tree and we had to rescue him.

- You're not making up this story, are you?

- I swear to God I am not.

- So, are you coming or not?

- You know what? What don't you come to my place and meet my friends?

- Well, sounds exciting, meeting my friend's friends the first night, we are taking a strong start.

- You'll see, they are adorable, and we are having one hell of a party right now.

- Ok darling, I grab a cab and I'm coming.

- Great! Thank you, Mila. Oh, and don't be afraid if you see a lot of people, I'll explain to you later. Bye.

*

The rest of the night was magical. I spoke to so many people, I heard so many stories that I can't recollect whose story belongs to whom. It was the most beautiful evening of my life, thanks to Randy, to his project. He has brought joy and kindness in the heart of all these people, and they came to tell him thank you. Thelma did what she does best, organizing things. She is a leader, a conductor and this reunion was her work, her masterpiece. She will continue to reunite people, to provoke meetings with her cat bar, "The meow". People will share a coffee or a milkshake, people will go there to find peace and rest, they will have the possibility to read some beautiful stories, a cat on their knees. The Meow is not a big place, Thelma creates it at her image, soft, discrete but full of promises.

I was happy to spend the evening (the night!) with Mila. She had been warmly welcomed. I guess she thought at first: "what the hell is going on here?", I am sure of it because when she finally saw me, she told "what the hell is going on here?". And then, she added "I knew you were a crazy woman, but that!"

We drank, we drank, and we drank! We danced a little and we sang... a lot! We stopped when we were too drunk to pursue. Maybe it was when the cops made their appearance, being called several times by some people in the neighborhood. But they didn't leave without taking a shot with us. Mila can be a very convincing woman. But it was when Thelma, who was beyond drunkenness, said "hey, who invited some strippers?", that we knew we drank too much. They left quickly and all shy.

I didn't go to bed, I watched the sunset on the roof, alone. I wanted to be alone for this moment. The apartment was empty. Everyone was gone, groups after groups. Mila left at five, she told me she needed to sleep a little bit before going to work. She had already skip her morning gym session to stay with me longer. I met a true friend and we already plan a karaoke night.

It is now 7 a.m. I have taken a long hot shower, invigorating shower. I feel ready to go through the day. I am drinking my coffee, still on the roof, watching the city, listening to the day began, I hear engines roaring, I hear people talking, music coming from unknown houses, I hear the traffic growing. It's good to hear the city waking up. I dressed, I took another coffee. I chatted a little with Randy. He is going to work, he is a substitute teacher for a month, his class is waiting for him. Thelma is still sleeping, with Sleepy, the little devil. She has still some time to sleep, her shop doesn't open before 11.

I feel suddenly a cold draught cross me. I am ready, I ate, I am dressed but for what? Where to go? What should I do? All of a sudden, I am lost again, the room starts spinning, I sat down and try to relax. The sun is warmly caressing my skin. I relax. I am the captain of myself again. I decide that the best thing to do is to go to the park, and why not take a milkshake, who cares? The day is beautiful, the weather is perfect, a walk will do me some good.

8 a.m. (the heart empty but heavy like a stone)

I am on my usual bench, sipping my cappuccino (yes, it was a bit too early for a milkshake, but it is not completely off the table). The park is not very crowded. I close my eyes, my head up towards the sun.

-       I never saw you so early.

I startle and open my eyes, trying to see who's talking to me. I see the old man in front of me, the one that is usually reading his newspaper on the bench next to mine. We never talk and a thousand times I created him a life. He has been a retired president, a murderer that was never caught or a widower remembering his passed away wife.

-       Sorry, I didn't mean to scare you.

-       No, no, it's nothing. I was just dreaming.

- We never talk, I didn't mean to bother you, but this is the first time I see you at such an hour, so... Well, I let you drink your coffee.

- You don't bother me. I am Rose by the way (stretching my hand to him).

- (we share a quick handshake) I am Burt.

- Do you want to sit with me?

- With pleasure, but are you sure I won't be bothering you?

- Burt, we see each other almost every day, I am glad you came to talk to me.

- Isn't it silly that we never talked before?

- I always wanted to, but I never dare.

- You were probably thinking "what if this guy is an old grumpy? What will I do the other days, that could be awkward!"

- It was something like that, yes.

- So, what brings you here so early?

- It's a long story Burt.

- As you know, I have plenty of time.

Burt and I talked for a while, about two hours. I told him what happened to me, he was a very good listener. It felt as if I was on a therapy. I know nothing about Burt's life, where he comes from, what was his job, whether he was married or not, not a thing. I don't know if we will talk again. Around 10, he left. He told me that he had an appointment he could not afford to miss. Burt is a kind person, he didn't try to give me advices, he said that I will be going through hard times in my life, but that it was unavoidable. He told me that we can't suffer all along, that at some point, things smothered and quelled. But he told me that he could see that I haven't been happy at my work for the past five years. It is true. I never was happy, I earned good money, but I never was happy. At some point, you must admit the fact that money isn't everything. Some people can pretend to be ok, and they have the strength to say: "I'm good with what I have, I won't take the risk to lose it". And, time goes by, and they keep going until retirement. But, I am not like that. It is not that I am special, it's just something that I can't control. I can't physically go to work every single day, doing something that doesn't challenge me, that doesn't bring me happiness at the end. I am ok with the idea of working hard, but I want my rewards at the end, which means that I want to go home at night and feel good about what I did. I want to feel proud. My job might be useless to others, it doesn't matter. It's like, you know, there is millions of bakers or bartenders in the world, and many of us think that those jobs are "easy", I mean you don't have to be highly educated to do them, you have to be a hard worker. But, there is baker and baker. You can be an ordinary baker. You do your job without passion, you just do it because you have to. And, on the other hand, there is the top baker, the one that is totally dedicated to his work, and every day he does his best. He tries new things, he takes risks in order to sell new and creative products to his costumers. He too has hard days or bad days at work, because sometimes, there is something wrong and there is nothing you can do about it. He will go through crisis, major ones, and small ones but he has find his place on earth. He is a baker and he can say it proudly. That's the difference. He is more like an artist at the end.

Two months have passed since my dismissal. Bradley was indeed a man of honor, he offers me two weeks of vacation, and I went to Paris with Thelma. Today, I am working in the main studio's coffee shop. I am not a waitress but a manager. First, when Bradley offers me the job, I was really disappointed, because I thought it was an unwanted job. But the truth is, I am good at it and I am still in touch with the movies. Actually, I have become a confidant for some costumers. I have the occasion to talk to tourists, technicians, actors, directors and yes, even the writers. Bradley comes every day for his coffee and he is always nice and talkative. He asks me my opinion on his new projects, and he listens to me.

I don't have the time anymore to go rest in the park with my milkshake, so I haven't talk to Burt again, but I intend to fix that as soon as possible. I am always hanging in the studios and everyone knows me and greets me. I am still the nice little girl, smiling to everybody for no apparent reason. I don't think I'll be able to change that aspect of my personality.

I still see Mila from time to time. Thelma is still at the head of the Meow and it is doing very well. She started to make pies and they are so delicious that I have convince my boss to sell them in the coffee shop where I work (which is called the "Casablanca" by the way). What can I say about Randy? He is still writing, he is now a permanent teacher, he teaches reading and writing to the little ones. I can't wait for Thelma and Randy to have babies but every time I bring up the subject, I see Randy get all red and Thelma is life-threatening me. OK, they're not ready but come on, I'll be a terrific aunt. But I give them a break. The other night, I hide their condoms, but I was the only one laughing, Thelma didn't speak to me for about a week after that, so... no more jokes like that.

I don't know what else to say... I am happy. I have my inner circle of friends, I have a job that I like, I am a more respected person, and that's the more important thing I guess. I am still looking for love, but who knows, that might be another story for another book!

And, I almost forgot! I am going to the gym so, no more reason for my dear narrator to call me "plump" in the future.

Rose, you still got some weight to...

Shut up! Just... Don't say one more word.

THE END

Hey, no! You don't the right to end my book like that! Can't you at least let me finish my book?

Come on, you've got something to say? The story is over.

You forgot to tell something.

What?

Randy's letters, they are not going to end on a shelf. Sure, they bring comfort to the customers of the "Meow", but you had an idea. You brought them to Bradley, and you made a deal with him: he gets the letters published and he can buy the rights. He has the opportunity to have a whole bank of stories at his disposal. It's a win-win deal.

Is Randy ok about that? I don't think he is the kind of guy running after the money.

No, but he gets published and that can be his chance to become a writer, or a screenwriter. Randy would never work for a major studio, but he could have some connections after that, an opportunity to be fully creative.

A teacher and a writer, I like that. And, that's the end of the story!

I WANT THE FINAL WORD!

You realize that you are fighting against your own character, that YOU created? You've got some problems man. You need some help. Give me some rest, give you some rest and get out for a walk. A walk, a milkshake and sex, in that order.

I'll do that.

© 2018, Merlet, Benjamin
Edition : Books on Demand,
12/14 rond-Point des Champs-Elysées, 75008 Paris
Impression : BoD - Books on Demand, Norderstedt, Allemagne
ISBN : 9782322120420
Dépôt légal : avril 2018